FACTS AT YOUR FINGERTIPS

INTRODUCING CHEMISTRY
CHEMICAL REACTIONS

HARVARD PUBLIC LIBRARY
4 POND ROAD
HARVARD, MA 01451

CONTENTS

What is a chemical reaction?	4–7
Chemical bonds	8–13
Types of reactions	14–19
Energy in chemical reactions	20–27
Heat and chemical reactions	28–35
Entropy and free energy	36–41
Rates of reactions	42–47
Catalysts	48–53
Electrochemistry	54–57
Nuclear reactions	58–61
Glossary	62
Further research	63
Index	64

Published by Brown Bear Books Limited

4877 N. Circulo Bujia
Tucson, AZ 85718
USA

and

First Floor
9-17 St. Albans Place
London N1 0NX
UK
www.brownreference.com

© 2010 The Brown Reference Group Ltd

Library of Congress Cataloging-in-Publication Data

Chemical reactions / edited by Graham Bateman.
  p. cm. — (Facts at your fingertips)
  Includes index.
  ISBN 978-1-936333-11-0 (lib. bdg.)
  1. Chemical reactions—Juvenile literature. I. Bateman, Graham.
  II. Title. III. Series.

QD501.C4645 2010
541'.39–dc22

2010016429

All rights reserved. This book is protected by copyright.
No part of it may be reproduced, stored in a retrieval system,
or transmitted in any form or by any means, without the prior permission
in writing of the publisher, nor be otherwise circulated in any form of
binding or cover other than that in which it is published and without a
similar condition including this condition being imposed on the
subsequent publisher.

ISBN-13 978-1-936333-11-0

Editorial Director: Lindsey Lowe
Project Director: Graham Bateman
Design Manager: David Poole
Designer: Steve McCurdy
Text Editors: Peter Lewis, Briony Ryles
Indexer: David Bennett
Children's Publisher: Anne O'Daly
Production Director: Alastair Gourlay

Printed in the United States of America

Picture Credits
Abbreviations: SS=Shutterstock; c=center; t=top; l=left; r=right.

Cover Images
Front: SS: Shemp R. Camp
Back: istockphoto: photointrigue

1 SS: Jafaris Mustafa; 3 SS: Tish 1; 4 SS: Roman Sigaev; 5 Photos.com; 8–9 SS: Higyou; 11 SS: Juan Vte. Munoz; 12 SS: Yury Kosourov;14 SS: Losevsky Pavel; 17 SS: Kamenetskiy Konstantin; 18 SS: Jafaris Mustafa; 20–21 SS: Arnold John Labrentz; 21 SS: Igor Kisselev; 22 Great Images in NASA; 23 Wikimedia Commons Protein Data Base; 25 SS: Olivier Le Queinec; 26 SS: Tish 1; 28 SS: Tom Oliviera; 28–29 SS: Matt Antonio; 30–31 SS: Hadrian; 33t SS: Lisa F. Young; 33b SS: Lev Dolgachov; 36–37 SS: Pavel Cheiko; 41 NASA/ESA J. Blakeslee and H. Ford (Johns Hopkins University); 42 SS: Ivan Cholakov Gostock; 48–49 SS: Cobalt 88; 49 SS: William alum; 51 NASA/Marshall Space Flight Center; 52 SS: Michael Zysman; 54–55 SS: Huguette Roe; 58 SS: Tatjana M.

Artwork © The Brown Reference Group Ltd

The Brown Reference Group Ltd has made every effort to trace copyright holders of the pictures used in this book. Anyone having claims to ownership not identified above is invited to contact The Brown Reference Group Ltd.

Facts at your Fingertips—Introducing Chemistry describes the essentials of chemistry from the fundamentals of atomic structure, through the periodic table, to descriptions of different types of reactions and the properties of elements, including industrial applications for chemical processes.

A chemical reaction is any process that changes one substance into another; it involves two basic components of the universe—energy and matter. *Chemical Reactions* describes the processes involved in chemical reactions, how energy and heat are involved, and what factors affect the speed of reaction, including the use of catalysts. Chemical reactions can also produce electricity. Nuclear reactions, which involve the release of enormous amounts of energy, are included as a special case.

Numerous explanatory diagrams and informative photographs, detailed features on related aspects of the topics covered and the main scientists involved in the advancement of chemistry, and definitions of key "Science Words," all enhance the coverage. "Try This" features outline experiments that can be undertaken as a first step to practical investigations.

WHAT IS A CHEMICAL REACTION?

What turns food into energy, coal into fire, and iron into rust? The answer is chemical reactions. Chemical reactions are taking place all around us and even inside our bodies.

Without chemical reactions, the world would be a very boring place. A chemical reaction is any process that changes one substance into another. Some reactions happen naturally, such as when we digest food or when metal objects become rusty. Other reactions are produced by people to improve their lives. For example, we burn fuel to heat our homes or power an automobile engine.

Reactions involve the interaction between two basic components of the universe—matter and energy. Scientists call any substance that takes up space matter. Rocks, water, and air are all made of matter. Energy is the ability to do work—to move or reshape matter in some way. Heat, light, and electricity are types of energy. During a chemical reaction, energy works to reorganize matter.

Inside matter

All matter on Earth is made of elements. An element cannot be reduced to a simpler substance. All elements are made of atoms. An atom is the smallest piece of an element that still has the properties of that element. Atoms do have smaller parts, which have other properties. Chemists represent each element with a symbol of one or two letters.

Atoms are often found in simple combinations called molecules. A pure substance consists of only one type of molecule, which is described by a molecular formula. The formula shows how many atoms of each element are involved. One of the simplest molecules is hydrogen (H_2). This formula shows that the molecule contains two hydrogen (H) atoms. The formula for water is H_2O; two hydrogen atoms are connected to one oxygen (O) atom.

CHEMISTRY AND LIFE

Life could not exist without chemical reactions. Like the bodies of all life-forms, the human body is powered by chemical reactions. You inhale oxygen (O_2) when you take a breath of air. And when you eat food, your stomach extracts useful chemicals, such as sugar, from it. Oxygen reacts with the sugars in your body to produce carbon dioxide (CO_2) and water (H_2O). Biologists call this chemical reaction respiration. The reaction releases energy from sugar, which keeps the body alive. You exhale the products of respiration with each breath.

Plants complete the same chemical reaction in reverse—a process called photosynthesis. The plants take in carbon dioxide and water, and use the energy found in sunlight to produce oxygen and sugar.

CHEMICAL REACTIONS

All chemical reactions involve change. Burning is one way of converting chemicals such as coal or oil into other compounds, releasing energy that can be used to power engines or provide heat.

Chemical reaction ingredients

The substances you start with in a chemical reaction are called the reactants. The new substances that are created are called the products. Chemists write the reactants and products as chemical equations. All chemical equations follow the same format: Reactants → Products. Numbers are used in the equation to indicate how much of each substance is needed. The arrow indicates that a chemical reaction has taken place and a new chemical has been produced.

A simple chemical reaction occurs when carbon dioxide (CO_2) forms. This molecule contains carbon (C) and oxygen atoms. These two elements combine to produce carbon dioxide. The equation of this reaction looks like this:

$$C + O_2 \rightarrow CO_2$$

A balanced chemical equation shows exactly how much of the reactant and product are involved in the reaction. Chemists balance equations to determine how many reactants are needed to produce new substances. A balanced equation is one where the number of atoms on one side is the same as the number on the other.

Subatomic particles

The smaller parts of the atom are the pieces involved in a chemical reaction. These parts are called subatomic particles. At the center of the atom is the nucleus. The nucleus is a densely packed ball of positively charged particles called protons. These are mixed with neutral (noncharged) particles called neutrons.

Opposite charges attract, while like charges repel. The positively charged protons in the nucleus attract negatively charged particles called electrons. Electrons are much smaller than protons. They move in clouds around the nucleus. It is the electrons that allow an atom to form bonds with other atoms. How the electrons from two atoms interact determines which type of bond forms. Electrons can be given, taken, or shared to create a bond between two or more atoms. During a chemical reaction, bonds linking some atoms are broken and new bonds are built between others. When atoms of different elements bond they create a substance called a compound. Compounds often look very different from the reactants that produced them.

EVERYDAY CHEMISTRY

Using chemical reactions, chemists have created countless products we use everyday. Look around your home and you are bound to see many. Plastics are chains of different types of chemicals strung together. Soaps and toothpastes are made from fatty substances using chemical reactions. And recipes tell us how to use chemical reactions to cook food. Chemical reactions are everywhere.

Dish soap used to clean dirty pans and plates is produced by a chemical reaction.

WHAT IS A CHEMICAL REACTION?

For example, sugar is a compound of carbon, hydrogen, and oxygen. Pure hydrogen and oxygen are both invisible gases and pure carbon forms diamonds, or graphite, the substance used as pencil lead. Together these elements form many compounds called carbohydrates. These include the sweet-tasting crystals known as sugar.

Inside energy

Energy is an essential part of chemical reactions. It is required to break a chemical bond, and energy is released when another bond forms. Heat is one type of energy often involved in chemical reactions. Some reactions will take in heat. Other chemical reactions will give off heat, such as burning fuel.

Putting it all together

When compounds undergo a chemical reaction, energy works to rearrange the bonds between the atoms. For example, consider the equation: $AB + C \rightarrow A + BC$.

Elements A and B are bonded to form the AB compound. The AB compound and C are the reactants. During the reaction, the bond between A and B breaks and a bond between B and C is built. A and the BC compound are the products.

In this reaction, one bond was broken and a new bond between two different atoms was made. The atoms themselves did not change—A did not change to D, for instance. The reaction changed only how the elements were joined.

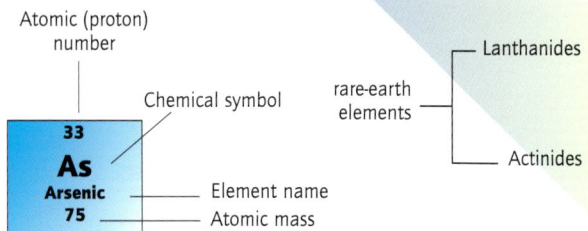

CHEMICAL REACTIONS

SCIENCE WORDS

- **Atom:** The smallest piece of an element that still retains the properties of that element.
- **Chemical reaction:** A process in which atoms of different elements join together or break apart.
- **Element:** A substance made up of just one type of atom.
- **Matter:** Anything that can be weighed.

The periodic table

The periodic table—shown below—is an organized list providing information about individual and groups of elements. The vertical columns are called groups, or families, of elements. Members of each group usually react in the same way.

Each group has a set of known properties. For example, the column on the left of the periodic table is known as the alkali metals. These are very reactive elements, such as sodium and potassium. Instead of memorizing the properties for every element, chemists simply consult the periodic table.

Legend:
- ACTINIDES
- NOBLE GASES
- NONMETALS
- METALLOIDS
- HYDROGEN
- ALKALI METALS
- ALKALINE-EARTH METALS
- METALS
- LANTHANIDES

Group 10	Group 11	Group 12	Group 13	Group 14	Group 15	Group 16	Group 17	Group 18
								2 **He** Helium 4
			5 **B** Boron 11	6 **C** Carbon 12	7 **N** Nitrogen 14	8 **O** Oxygen 16	9 **F** Fluorine 19	10 **Ne** Neon 20
			13 **Al** Aluminium 27	14 **Si** Silicon 28	15 **P** Phosphorus 31	16 **S** Sulfur 32	17 **Cl** Chlorine 35	18 **Ar** Argon 40
28 **Ni** Nickel 59	29 **Cu** Copper 64	30 **Zn** Zinc 65	31 **Ga** Gallium 70	32 **Ge** Germanium 73	33 **As** Arsenic 75	34 **Se** Selenium 79	35 **Br** Bromine 80	36 **Kr** Krypton 84
46 **Pd** Palladium 106	47 **Ag** Silver 108	48 **Cd** Cadmium 112	49 **In** Indium 115	50 **Sn** Tin 119	51 **Sb** Antimony 122	52 **Te** Tellurium 128	53 **I** Iodine 127	54 **Xe** Xenon 131
78 **Pt** Platinum 195	79 **Au** Gold 197	80 **Hg** Mercury 201	81 **Tl** Thallium 204	82 **Pb** Lead 207	83 **Bi** Bismuth 209	84 **Po** Polonium (209)	85 **At** Astatine (210)	86 **Rn** Radon (222)
110 **Ds** Darmstadtium (281)	111 **Rg** Roentgenium (280)	112 **Cn** Copernicium (285)	113 **Uut** Ununtrium (284)	114 **Uuq** Ununquadium (289)	115 **Uup** Ununpentium (291)	116 **Uuh** Ununhexium (293)	117 **Uus** Ununseptium (295)	118 **Uuo** Ununoctium (294)

Lanthanides:

62 **Sm** Samarium 150	63 **Eu** Europium 152	64 **Gd** Gadolinium 157	65 **Tb** Terbium 159	66 **Dy** Dysprosium 163	67 **Ho** Holmium 165	68 **Er** Erbium 167	69 **Tm** Thulium 169	70 **Yb** Ytterbium 173	71 **Lu** Lutetium 175

Actinides:

94 **Pu** Plutonium (244)	95 **Am** Americium (243)	96 **Cm** Curium (247)	97 **Bk** Berkelium (247)	98 **Cf** Californium (251)	99 **Es** Einsteinium (252)	100 **Fm** Fermium (257)	101 **Md** Mendelevium (258)	102 **No** Nobelium (259)	103 **Lr** Lawrencium (260)

CHEMICAL BONDS

Chemical bonds allow atoms to stick together in different combinations. How a bond between atoms forms depends on the number and location of the atom's electrons.

Chemical bonds are created when atoms give, take, or share electrons. There are three types of chemical bonds: ionic, covalent, and metallic. The type of bond formed between atoms depends on how many electrons they have in the atom and how they are arranged.

Electron locations

The location of electrons in an atom is one factor that determines how that atom will form bonds. Scientists use two models to explain the location of electrons in the atom—the Bohr model and the quantum mechanics model.

The Bohr model describes electrons orbiting (circling) the nucleus of an atom like the planets orbit the Sun. As electrons travel in circles around the nucleus, they are held in place by the pull of the nucleus. The nucleus has a positive charge, which attracts the negative charges of the electrons. This model for the atom works well for very simple atoms, such as hydrogen.

The quantum mechanics model is more modern and mathematical. It describes volumes of space called electron clouds, inside which electrons reside. It is not

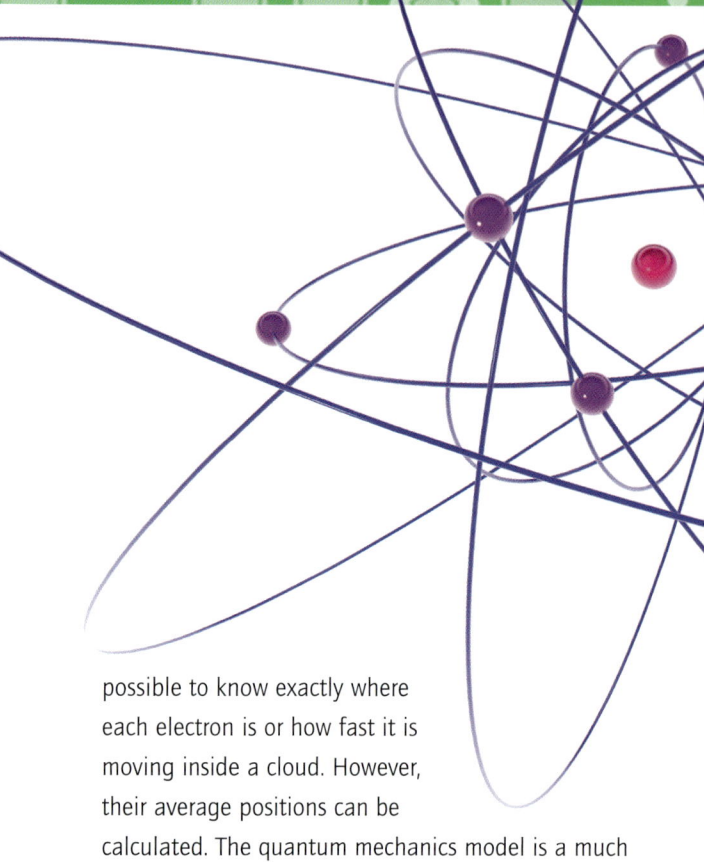

possible to know exactly where each electron is or how fast it is moving inside a cloud. However, their average positions can be calculated. The quantum mechanics model is a much more complicated and more accurate way of describing how an atom is put together than the Bohr model.

Energy levels

In both models, electrons sit at different energy levels. An energy level determines how likely an electron is to be involved in a chemical reaction and form a bond. Electrons in energy levels farthest from the nucleus are most likely to become involved in a reaction because they are held only weakly by the nucleus.

Atoms can have several energy levels. The level closest to the nucleus can only hold two electrons. Chemists call this the lowest energy level. The levels farther from the nucleus can hold more than two electrons. Electrons need more energy to sit in the outer energy levels.

The energy levels are sometimes called orbitals—the areas in which electrons orbit around the nucleus. Chemists also describe them as electron shells because they can be thought of as layers, or shells, surrounding the nucleus.

SCIENCE WORDS

- **Metal:** A hard but flexible element. Metals are good conductors. Their atoms have only a few outer electrons.
- **Metalloid:** An element that has both metallic and nonmetallic properties.
- **Nonmetal:** An element that is not a metal. Nonmetals are poor conductors. Their atoms tend to have several outer electrons.

CHEMICAL REACTIONS

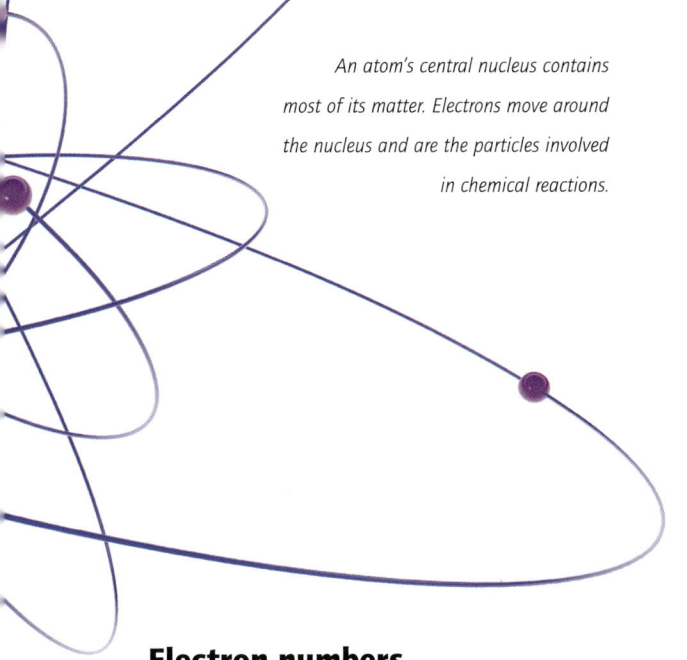

An atom's central nucleus contains most of its matter. Electrons move around the nucleus and are the particles involved in chemical reactions.

> ### John Dalton
>
> English chemist John Dalton (1766–1844) is best known for his atomic theory—a basic set of rules that explain how atoms behave, including how they combine with each other. Four of Dalton's rules are still true today: 1) All matter is composed of atoms; 2) All atoms in an element are the same; 3) Atoms combine to form compounds; 4) Atoms are rearranged in a chemical reaction. Only a final rule—that atoms cannot be divided into smaller particles—was wrong. We now know atoms contain even smaller pieces.

Electron numbers

The number of electrons in an atom is the other factor that determines how that atom will react and form bonds. An atom is most stable (unreactive) when its shells are full of electrons. An atom with a full shell will not give, take, or share electrons easily. Because of that, the atom does not get involved in chemical reactions and form bonds.

Electrons fill the inner shells first. The lowest-energy shell has space for just two electrons. Helium atoms have two electrons, and these fill the inner shell. This makes the atom stable. It does not give, take, or share electrons because its shell is full.

Larger atoms have two or more electron shells. The extra shells are larger than the first one and need eight electrons to become stable. Becoming stable with eight electrons is called the octet rule. This rule drives all chemical reactions because atoms will react with each other until they become stable.

Stable atoms are unreactive. Atoms with incomplete outer shells will give, take, or share electrons to fill their energy levels. These atoms are reactive because they take part in chemical reactions. An atom with one electron in its outer shell will give it away easily. Atoms with six or seven outer electrons readily take electrons to fill that shell.

When atoms give, take, or share electrons they create bonds. During a chemical reaction, bonds are broken and built to create new molecules.

Atoms and bonds

Atoms have a naturally neutral charge. The positive protons in the nucleus balance out the negative electrons in orbit around them. Because of the location and number of electrons, some atoms create bonds more readily than others. Based on this ability to form bonds, all elements can be divided into three basic types: metals, nonmetals, and metalloids.

Metal atoms have only a few outer electrons and tend to lose them during chemical reactions. Most elements are metals, and they have certain properties. Metals are solid, shiny, and can conduct electricity. A solid piece of metal contains many free-floating electrons shared among the atoms. These electrons act like stepping stones for an electric charge within the metal, allowing the charge to move within the solid. This property makes metals good materials to use in wires and electric cables.

Nonmetals are the opposite of metals. Nonmetals tend to gain electrons in chemical reactions. They come in all forms and may be liquid, gas, or solid in normal conditions. They are not good at conducting electricity. There are no free-floating electrons to help

CHEMICAL BONDS

>
> ## TRY THIS
>
> **Rusting nails**
>
> Place an iron nail in a jar. Cover the nail completely with water and add two tablespoons of salt. Put the lid on the jar. Come back and check the nail in about an hour. What do you see? You are watching a chemical reaction in action:
>
> iron + oxygen → iron oxide
>
> A new ionic bond between iron and oxygen forms to create iron oxide, or rust. Salt and water help the reaction go faster. The rust should look like dark, reddish spots on the nail.
>
>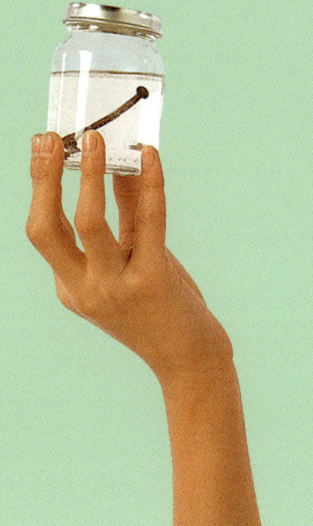
>
> *When it gets wet, iron reacts with oxygen to form rust, a red, flaky iron oxide.*

move an electric charge. Instead, nonmetals are good insulators. Metalloids are semiconductors, which change from being insulators to conductors depending on the conditions.

How strongly an atom holds onto its electrons and pulls electrons away from another atom is called its electronegativity. Nonmetals are more electronegative than metals. Metal atoms have only a few outer electrons, which the atoms give away easily.

Ionic bonds

During a chemical reaction, three types of bonds can form: ionic, covalent, or metallic. An ionic bond occurs when a metal atom gives an electron to a nonmetal atom. The atom that gives away an electron loses a negative charge and becomes positively charged itself.

Chemists call atoms that have become charged in this way ions. A positively charged ion is a cation. The atom that takes an electron receives an extra negative charge and becomes a negatively charged ion, or anion. Opposite charges attract each other, so the cation and anion join to form an ionic bond. Bonded ions are called ionic compounds.

A common ionic compound is table salt, formed when sodium (Na) bonds with chlorine (Cl). Sodium is a typical metal. It is silvery and conductive, with one electron to give. Chlorine is a nonmetal gas, in need of one electron to complete its octet and become stable.

Put sodium and chlorine in a container together, and sodium will lose its electron and become a cation (Na^+). Chlorine takes the same electron and becomes an anion (Cl^-). The Na^+ bonds with the Cl^- to form NaCl (sodium chloride), or the table salt we use in food.

All ionic molecules are formed by cations and anions bonding. This gives the molecules a positively charged end, or pole, and a negatively charged pole. Each pole is attracted to another with the opposite charge on a different molecule. As a result, ionic molecules tend to join up in regular patterns, called crystals. Because each molecule is held firmly in place by all the other molecules around it, ionic crystals tend to be hard solids that do not bend or break easily.

Because of the strength of the attraction between ions, it takes a lot of energy to pull them apart. Heating the solid provides enough energy to pull some of the molecules apart and they melt into a liquid. The temperature at which a substance melts is called its melting point. Further heating separates the molecules more until the liquid boils to produce a gas. The temperature when this happens is called the boiling point. Ionic compounds tend to have high melting and boiling points.

When an ionic compound is dissolved in water, the ions separate and float freely in the water. These floating ions can carry electricity through the water. The ability to conduct electricity when dissolved or melted is another common property of ionic compounds.

CHEMICAL REACTIONS

Sand (silicon dioxide) and water are two of the most common compounds on the surface of Earth. Both are covalent compounds. However, silicon dioxide forms hard crystals, while water is a liquid.

Covalent bonds

A covalent bond is formed when two nonmetal atoms share their electrons to become stable. Instead of one electron moving into the outer shell of another atom, the shells overlap to share the electron. Each electron becomes bonded to both the nuclei.

A group of atoms held together with bonds like this is called a covalent molecule. Hydrogen atoms form the simplest covalent molecules. Hydrogen has only a single electron and only needs two electrons to become stable (instead of eight). A hydrogen atom shares its electron with another hydrogen atom, forming a H_2 molecule. Hydrogen is found in nature as H_2. Six other elements form molecules in a similar way: oxygen (O_2), nitrogen (N_2), fluorine (F_2), chlorine (Cl_2), bromine (Br_2), and iodine (I_2).

Because all covalent bonds involve the sharing of electrons, covalent compounds tend to have similar properties. The crystals of covalent compounds fall into two types. The first type is similar to an ionic crystal because all the atoms are connected to each other by a strong bond. This is the case with diamond, which is an extremely hard form of pure carbon. Diamond is the

ELECTRON DOTS

Chemists show how atoms form bonds by drawing atoms in a simple way. The nucleus is a central circle and is surrounded by layers of electrons. During chemical reactions, electrons move between atoms or are shared in the outer shells of two atoms. The diagram below shows how an electron moves from a sodium atom to a chlorine atom to make sodium and chloride ions. The ions bond together to make sodium chloride, or common salt.

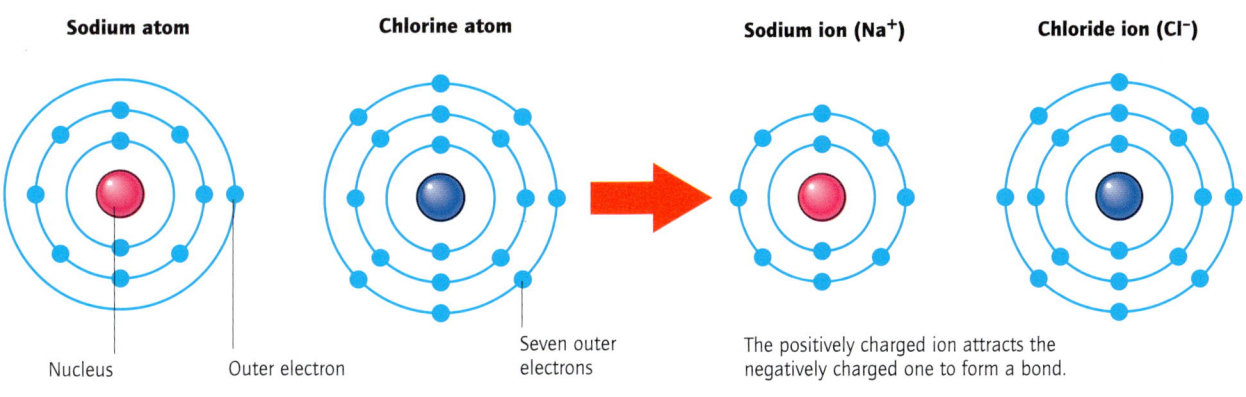

11

CHEMICAL BONDS

An electric cable designed to carry electric currents. Copper wires carry the current. Copper is one of the most conductive metals. Plastic, made from nonmetal elements, does not conduct electricity. Plastic surrounds copper so the electric current is kept safely inside.

hardest substance known. Silicon dioxide—the scientific name for sand and quartz—also forms hard crystals in this way. Both diamond and silicon dioxide have high melting and boiling points because of the strong network of bonds inside their crystals.

The other types of covalent compounds do not form crystals in the same way. They have no strong forces to bond molecules to each other. Instead only weak forces, called van der Waals forces, pull molecules together. Because these forces are so weak, solids are only formed at very cold temperatures. In normal conditions, the covalent compounds are gases or liquids. For example, carbon dioxide is normally a gas and will only form a crystal at very low temperatures.

Because electrons are shared in covalent compounds, there are no free-floating charged particles to conduct electricity. As a result, covalent compounds tend to be good insulators.

Covalent compounds that include carbon (C) and hydrogen (H) are called organic compounds. Many burn easily when exposed to oxygen and are used as fuels. Gasoline, for example, is a mixture of several organic compounds. The term organic is used for these compounds because many were originally made by living organisms.

Metallic bonds

Metals are generally hard solids. They tend to be flexible, too. The atoms are held together by metallic bonds, and a metal's properties are a result of these

---

ISOMER STRUCTURES

The compound C_3H_8O has three forms, or isomers. The isomers have different chemical properties. Two of them are types of alcohols while the other is an ether.

Propan-2-ol

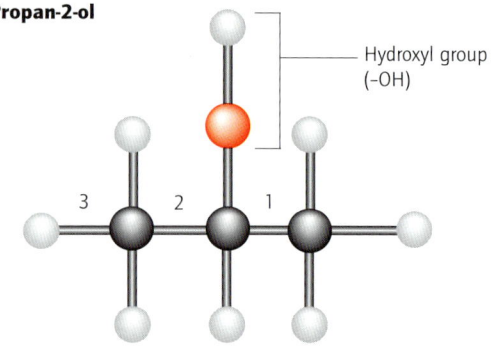

This alcohol molecule is called propan-2-ol because the hydroxyl is bonded to the second carbon (2) atom.

Propan-1-ol

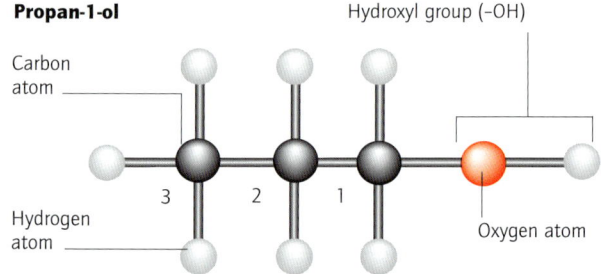

This alcohol molecule is called propan-1-ol. The hydroxyl group, which all alcohols have, is attached to the first carbon (1) atom.

Methyl-ethyl ether

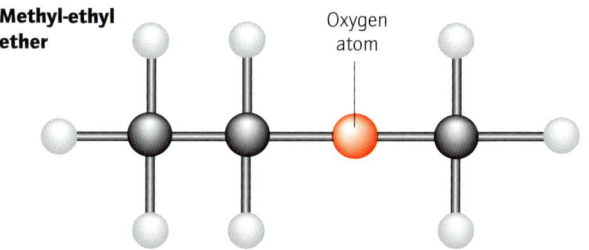

The third isomer is not an alcohol. Instead the oxygen atom is bonded to two carbon atoms. Molecules like this are called ethers.

CHEMICAL REACTIONS

bonds. Metallic bonds occur when metal atoms share a pool of electrons. Unlike a covalent bond, where electrons are shared but still bound to a nucleus, electrons in a metallic bond are free to move around.

A piece of solid silver consists of atoms floating in a pool of free electrons. All the metal atoms give away their single outer electron, which make up a negatively charged pool of electrons. This negative charge is attracted to the positive charge of the atoms' nuclei. This attraction bonds the metal atoms together.

Although metallic bonds make most metals hard solids, they also allow the atoms inside to move past each other. This property is what makes metals ductile and malleable. Ductile solids can be pulled into thin wires, and malleable ones flattened into sheets. The pool of electrons holds the metal atoms together as the solid is reshaped and prevents the solid from breaking.

Isomers

Isomers are molecules that contain the same atoms, but are arranged in different ways. They have the same chemical formula, but have a different shape. Understanding isomers is important in chemical reactions because isomers have different atoms available for bonding.

Good examples of isomers are the organic compounds with the formula C_3H_8O. These molecules take three forms (see left). Two are a type of alcohol and are known as propanols. Alcohols are a group of organic compounds. Alcoholic drinks contain an alcohol called ethanol, but all other alcohols are extremely poisonous. In propanol molecules, the oxygen atom is bonded to any of the three carbon atoms and to a hydrogen atom. Together the hydrogen and oxygen form a hydroxyl group (–OH). All alcohols have a hydroxyl group, which plays a role in chemical reactions. The two C_3H_8O alcohols are called propan-1-ol and propan-2-ol.

In the third C_3H_8O molecule the oxygen bonds between two carbons. This compound is not an alcohol. Instead it is an ether called methyl-ethyl ether. Ethers react in a different way from alcohols.

TRY THIS

Moving metals
Sand the edge of a penny so the outer layer of copper is rubbed away exposing zinc underneath. Place the penny in a pint of vinegar for one hour. Now remove the penny and add 1.5 ounces (50 g) of Epsom salts and 2 ounces (60 g) of sugar to the vinegar. Use alligator clips to attach electrical wires to the sanded penny and a new, clean penny. Lower the pennies into the vinegar, making sure they do not touch. Connect the clean penny to the negative terminal of a large battery. Connect the sanded penny to the positive terminal. After 10 minutes, the clean penny should have a dark, silvery coating of zinc on it.

You used electricity to break the metallic bonds between copper and zinc on the sanded penny. The vinegar, salts, and sugar helped move the zinc from the positively charged penny to the negatively charged penny. Scientists call this electroplating.

An electric current flows between the two pennies through the mixture of vinegar, salts, and sugar. The zinc is carried by this current from the sanded penny to the other coin. This zinc forms a very thin layer on the second coin, giving it a new silvery color.

Zinc-coated penny

New penny

TYPES OF REACTIONS

Chemists classify chemical reactions according to how chemical bonds are broken or built. Then the scientists write down those reactions as chemical equations.

Chemical reactions occur when new bonds are formed between atoms to create new compounds. Chemists have names for many different types of chemical reactions. The type of chemical reaction depends on how the reactants change to make the products. The five main types of chemical reactions are combination, decomposition, displacement, redox, and combustion reactions. Remember these are general groups, and it is possible for a chemical reaction to be a member of more than one group at the same time.

Some elements are involved in nuclear reactions. These are very different from chemical reactions. Instead of rearranging the bonds to form new compounds, a nuclear reaction actually changes the atom, making one element into another.

Combination reactions

A combination reaction occurs when two or more reactants combine to form one product: A + B → AB. In more complex cases where there are several reactants,

Chemical reactions can involve reactants and products in all states. For example, reacting liquids can produce gases.

more than one product can be formed by this type of reaction. Common compounds, such as water, carbon dioxide, and common salt are all the products of combination reactions.

When carbon burns it is taking part in a simple combination reaction. Oxygen combines with the carbon, producing carbon dioxide gas and some heat. The chemical equation representing this is:

$$C + O_2 \rightarrow CO_2$$

This is also an example of a combustion reaction and a redox reaction.

> ### SCIENCE WORDS
>
> - **Dissolve:** To form a solution.
> - **Insoluble:** A substance that cannot dissolve.
> - **Precipitate:** An insoluble solid formed by a double displacement reaction between two dissolved compounds.
> - **Solute:** The substance that dissolves in a solvent.
> - **Solution:** A mixture that contains a dissolved substance. Solids usually dissolve in liquids.
> - **Solvent:** The liquid that solutes dissolve in.

CHEMICAL REACTIONS

Decomposition reactions

A decomposition reaction is the opposite of a combination reaction. It occurs when a single compound breaks down into two or more simpler substances: AB → A + B.

When you open a can of soda, carbon dioxide bubbles are formed by a decomposition reaction. The soda contains carbonic acid (H_2CO_3) dissolved in water. This mixture is squeezed inside a soda can under high pressure. When the can is opened, the pressure inside drops. This causes the acid to decompose and form water and bubbles of carbon dioxide gas that give the soda its refreshing taste. The decomposition reaction looks like this:

$H_2CO_3 \rightarrow H_2O + CO_2$

Displacement reactions

A displacement reaction occurs when a more reactive atom replaces a less active atom in a compound: A + BC → AB + C. A reactive atom is one that forms bonds easily. Chemists divide displacement reactions into two types: single and double displacements.

A single displacement reaction occurs when the reactive atom doing the replacing is an element. A double displacement occurs when the atom doing the replacing is already combined in another compound.

Double displacement reactions often happen in solutions. A solution is a mixture in which a solid is spread out evenly in a liquid until it has disappeared. This process is known as dissolving. Seawater is a solution of salt.

Double displacements are either in the form of precipitation reactions or neutralization reactions. In a precipitation reaction, one product is a compound that cannot dissolve. Instead it forms a precipitate, a solid that is separate from the solution. Precipitates eventually sink to the bottom of the solution.

In neutralization, one of the products is always water. The compounds that undergo neutralization reactions are called acids and bases. Acids are compounds that contain hydrogen ions (H^+). Bases contain negative hydroxide ions (OH^-). When acids and bases react they form water and another compound. This second product is neither an acid nor base and is described as neutral.

A neutralization occurs when you add household ammonia (a base; NH_4OH) to vinegar (an acid; CH_3O_2H). The vinegar's H^+ ions and the ammonia's OH^- ions combine to form water (H_2O). The NH_4^+ ion bonds with the vinegar ion (CH_3CO_4-). This forms ammonium ethanoate ($NH_4CH_3CO_2$), a neutral compound.

Redox reactions

A redox reaction occurs when electrons move from one of the reactants to the other. Combination, combustion, and single displacement reactions are also considered redox reactions. The word redox is short for "reduction-oxidation." Each redox reaction involves two separate reactions that occur at the same time. One half of the reaction occurs when one compound gains electrons. Chemists say an atom that has gained electrons has been reduced. The other half of this reaction, which happens at the same time, occurs

Robert Boyle

Robert Boyle (1627–1691) was one of the first chemists. His work helped future scientists figure out what was happening during chemical reactions. He was born in Ireland, but lived in England. He became interested in chemicals as he looked for a way of turning common metals into gold. He failed, but learned several things in the process. In 1661, Boyle published *The Skeptical Chemist*, in which he suggested that matter was made of many elements. Before this, people thought the only elements were earth, wind, water, and fire. Boyle also showed how gases changed as they were heated and squeezed. A hot gas takes up more room than a cold gas. In addition, when a gas is squeezed it gets hotter. This relationship is called Boyle's law. The law helped later chemists understand what gases are made of.

TYPES OF REACTIONS

TRY THIS

Testing for acid

Chemists use a substance called an indicator to test if something is an acid or a base. The indicator changes color when acid or bases are added to it. You can make an indicator at home from red cabbage.

Chop up a whole red cabbage into small pieces. Boil the pieces for 30 minutes. (Ask an adult to help you and be careful with the hot water.) The boiling cabbage will make the water turn red. Let the water cool and then use a sieve (strainer) to separate the cabbage from the water.

Put the red water in two cups. Add a teaspoon of baking soda to one of the cups. Baking soda is a base. Add a teaspoon of vinegar to the other cup. Vinegar is an acid. What colors do you see? Try testing other substances to see whether they are acids or bases.

Acid   Base

Boiling red cabbage makes a substance called anthocyanin mix into the water. The color of the anthocyanin depends on how many hydrogen ions are also in the mixture. Acids have many hydrogen ions, while bases do not have any.

when another compound loses electrons. Chemists say an atom that has lost electrons has been oxidized.

The burning of hydrogen is a redox reaction. The two halves of the reactions are written with the following equations:

$2H_2 \rightarrow 4H^+ + 4$ electrons

$O_2 + 4$ electrons $\rightarrow 2O^{2-}$

The two halves are combined into:

$2H_2 + O_2 \rightarrow 2H_2O$

The hydrogens have given their electrons to the oxygens and have been oxidized. The oxygens have gained electrons from the hydrogens and have been reduced.

Combustion reactions

A combustion reaction occurs when a compound reacts with the oxygen in the air and burns, producing flames and heat. Combustion reactions are often used by people to release heat.

Compounds known as hydrocarbons are often burned in combustion reactions. The name hydrocarbon is

The color of an indicator depends on how many hydrogen ions (H^+) are present. Chemists measure the amount of H^+ in a solution as its pH (= "potential hydrogen"). A solution with a low pH has a lot of hydrogen ions in it. Acids have a low pH. Bases have a high pH. Instead of H^+ ions, they have a large number of hydroxide ions (OH^-). When OH^- and H^+ ions meet they combine into water (H_2O). Water is neutral—it is not an acid or a base. It has a pH of 7. Anything with a pH below 7 is an acid. Bases have a pH of more than 7.

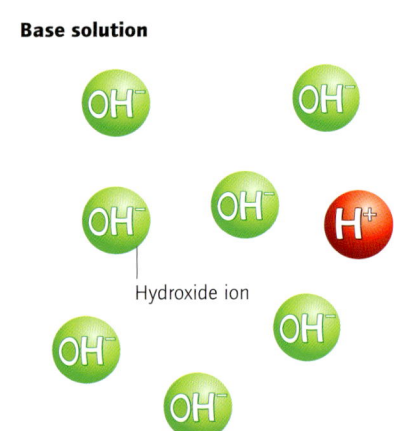

CHEMICAL REACTIONS

used because the compounds are made from carbon (C) and hydrogen (H). For example, propane gas (C_3H_8) is burned in cooking stoves to produce heat for cooking food. The reaction looks like this:

$$C_3H_8 + 5O_2 \rightarrow 3CO_2 + 4H_2O$$

Hydrocarbon fuels are extracted from petroleum oil and natural gas. They are often called fossil fuels because they are the remains of plants and other living things buried millions of years ago.

Chemical equations

Chemical equations can be written simply, with only the most necessary information. They can also be written in detail, giving much more information about what happens and what is needed for a reaction to happen.

A simple example of a chemical equation is when two hydrogen atoms combine: $H + H \rightarrow H_2$. This equation shows that two hydrogen atoms (H) combine into a hydrogen molecule (H_2).

A more detailed chemical equation might include other symbols, letters, and numbers. Much of this extra information added by these symbols is obvious to chemists or is not vital, so such symbols are not always included in equations. However the symbols can add useful information about how to perform the reaction successfully. A vertical arrow pointing up indicates that a product will form a gas that will bubble out of solution. Carbon dioxide gas is a product of several decomposition reactions and is indicated like this: $CO_2\uparrow$ An arrow pointing down indicates that a product will form as a precipitate and sink to the bottom of a liquid. Metals, including silver (Ag), often precipitate in displacement reactions and are indicated like this: $Ag\downarrow$

A two-headed arrow between the reactants and the products indicates that the reaction can go in both directions easily. Instead of writing two equations: $A + B \rightarrow AB$ and $AB \rightarrow A + B$, chemists combine the two: $A + B \rightleftarrows AB$.

> ### SCIENCE WORDS
> - **Chemical equation:** Symbols and numbers that show how reactants change into products during a reaction.
> - **Chemical formula:** A combination of chemical symbols that shows the type and number of elements in a molecule. H_2O is the formula for water, which contains two hydrogen (H) atoms and one oxygen (O).
> - **Chemical symbol:** Letters used to represent a certain element, such as O for oxygen or Na for sodium.
> - **Coefficient:** A number placed in front of a chemical formula to show how many molecules are used or produced by a reaction. $3H_2O$ stands for three water molecules.

In a detailed chemical equation letters in parentheses are used to indicate the state of matter of each compound. A solid is indicated with (s), a liquid with (l), and a gas with (g). When a chemical is dissolved in water, it is described as aqueous (from *aqua* the Latin for "water") and is indicated with (aq).

Sometimes it is easy to predict the states of matter involved in an equation, but not always. Water is usually in liquid form: $H_2O(l)$. However, water involved in reactions with a lot of heat often turns into a gas: $H_2O(g)$. To chemists, the numbers are the most important parts of a chemical equation.

Using numbers

A balanced equation tells you how much of the reactants are needed to produce a certain amount of the products. Chemists alter the amount of a reactant added to a reaction to predict how much of a product will be created.

Apples turn brown due to redox reactions.

17

TYPES OF REACTIONS

When you read a chemical equation, you see two types of numbers, but only one of these can be changed by the chemist. The small number to the lower right of an element indicates how many atoms are needed. For example, the "2" in H_2O shows that there are two hydrogen atoms in a molecule of water. There is also one oxygen atom but the "1" is never written. If you do not see a number, you can assume there is only one atom. Chemists can never change the small numbers in a compound in order to balance an equation, because that would imply different bonds between the atoms.

The larger number to the left of a compound is called a coefficient. The coefficient tells you how many of those molecules are needed. For example, $3H_2O$ means there are three water molecules taking part in the reaction. You can multiply the coefficient by the number of atoms present in each molecule to count the total number of atoms. In this case there are six hydrogen atoms (3 x 2) and three oxygen atoms (3 x 1).

Balancing equations

Chemists balance equations by changing the coefficients so that the number of atoms in the reactants equals the number in the products. For example, the equation for making hydrogen molecules, $H + H \rightarrow H_2$, is balanced because the number of atoms is the same on both sides. However the equation for reacting hydrogen with oxygen to make water is more complex. Both hydrogen and oxygen exist as molecules of two atoms: H_2 and O_2. Water contains atoms of both elements, but the simple equation $H_2 + O_2 \rightarrow H_2O$ does not balance. There is one oxygen atom in the product, but two oxygen atoms used as the reactants.

To balance this equation, you would add a coefficient to the reactants to match the number of atoms in the products: $2H_2 + O_2 \rightarrow 2H_2O$. Now the number of atoms is the same in the reactants and the products.

Balancing table

The chemical reaction to make water is fairly simple, so balancing the equation is easy. When equations get

The balloons float because they contain helium gas. Helium atoms are smaller and lighter than the atoms in the air. A mole of helium contains the same number of atoms as a mole of another element, but weighs much less.

more complicated, it can be helpful to draw a table to help you balance numbers in the reactants and products. The table lists the number of atoms of each element. Here is a table for $2H_2 + O_2 \rightarrow 2H_2O$:

	Reactants	Products
H	2 x 2 = 4	2 x 2 = 4
O	1 x 2 = 2	2 x 1 = 2

It is clear that you have a balanced equation because there are four atoms of hydrogen and two atoms of oxygen in both the reactants and the products.

When you balance an equation, you add or change coefficients until the numbers of atoms on both sides of the table match.

CHEMICAL REACTIONS

Now try to balance this equation of the reaction between phosphorus (P_4) and oxygen (O_2):

$P_4 + O_2 \rightarrow P_2O_5$

This equation has an unbalanced number of atoms.

	Reactants	Products
P	4	2
O	2	5

To balance the equation, first look at the most complicated compound (P_2O_5) and add a coefficient of 2. This gives you four phosphorus atoms and ten oxygen atoms in the products. Now balance the reactants. Oxygen molecules (O_2) each have two atoms, so five molecules would be needed to have ten atoms. Add a coefficient of 5 to the oxygen reactants. The reactants already have four phosphorus atoms, so you have finished. Using these numbers, the balanced equation would be:

$P_4 + 5O_2 \rightarrow 2P_2O_5$

The number of atoms is the same in the reactants and products, so the equation is balanced.

Balancing equations in reality

With a balanced equation, a chemist knows how many reactants are needed to create the products. However, you cannot count the number of atoms easily in a laboratory. Instead, chemists calculate the number of atoms in a substance by weighing it.

Atoms are counted in moles. The word mole represents a number: 602,213,670,000,000,000,000,000 (6.022×10^{23}). This number represents the number of atoms or molecules in a set weight of a compound. It is called Avogadro's number, and is named for Italian Amedeo Avogadro (1776–1856), who discovered that a set amount of any gas always contains the same number of atoms or molecules. On the periodic table, an element's atomic mass number is equal to the number of grams a mole of that element weighs. For example, helium has an atomic mass of 4. This means that one mole of helium weighs 4 grams (0.14 ounces).

TRY THIS

Redox in action

Photosynthesis is a redox reaction that occurs inside plants. You can watch it happening with a simple activity. Place a small piece of pondweed in a glass jar full of water. Cover the jar with a saucer and, holding them together, turn them upside down. Quickly fill the saucer with water to stop water leaking from the jar. A small amount of air should be trapped in the jar. Mark the level of the water with a pen. Now put the jar in a sunny place.

Soon there will be bubbles on the plant and the water level may have dropped slightly. The plant is using sunlight to react water with carbon dioxide to make oxygen and sugar. The sugar is the plant's food.

Photosynthesis produces bubbles of oxygen, which increase the amount of gas in the jar.

Compounds have molecular masses. That is the sum of all the atomic masses of the atoms inside a molecule. For example, the molecular mass of sodium chloride is roughly 58.5:23 for sodium and 35.5 for chlorine. So a mole of sodium chloride weighs 58.5 grams (2 ounces).

Chemists use these weights to measure exactly how much of an element or compound has been used up or produced in a reaction. That is the best way to figure out how the atoms have recombined to form compounds.

ENERGY IN CHEMICAL REACTIONS

When one substance changes into another, chemical reactions are happening. Some reactions take in energy, but others can give out energy in large amounts.

In the world around us, we can often see changes happening in familiar objects. Shiny metal objects may become dull and tarnished, and food may "go bad." Many of these changes involve chemical reactions.

Burning is a type of chemical reaction. In a forest fire, the burning trees gradually change into ash, smoke, and flames (which are hot, glowing gases). At the same time heat is produced.

Substances change in chemical reactions because atoms, the tiny particles with which matter is made, separate and rejoin in new ways. Wood, for example, is made up of a mixture of chemical compounds containing atoms of carbon and hydrogen, among others. During burning, these atoms separate and join with oxygen atoms from the air to form new compounds: the gases carbon dioxide and carbon monoxide, and water. The atoms themselves have changed very little in the process, but the ways in which they are grouped have changed.

CHEMICAL CHANGES

Chemical reactions are just one type of chemical change. When sugar dissolves in a cup of hot coffee, this, too, is a chemical change. The sugar seems to disappear, but really, the groups of atoms that make up the sugar simply spread out through the liquid. The sugar does not change into anything else it is just mixed very thoroughly with the liquid. So although it is a change, it is not usually called a reaction because the sugar does not change into a different compound.

Explaining chemical change

Chemists study why and how chemical compounds react with each other. They also investigate the effect of changes in temperature, pressure, and other conditions. They try to explain why some reactions happen faster than others, and why some need flames, sparks, or other types of extra help to get them started.

For example, the compound methane, which is made up of carbon and hydrogen atoms, can be burned in a kitchen oven to provide heat. During burning, the carbon and hydrogen atoms join with oxygen atoms from the air, forming carbon dioxide and water. Once the burning has been started with a

CHEMICAL REACTIONS

Forest fires are chemical reactions that often occur in hot, dry weather. Once the fire starts, it can take weeks to die down.

match or a switch on the oven, it will continue as long as the supply of methane and air lasts.

Iron also combines with oxygen in the air. An old iron nail, left out in the weather, becomes rusty. The rust consists of iron combined with oxygen. This reaction is similar to the burning of wood or methane, but happens much more slowly. It also needs no spark or flame to start it, unlike burning methane.

How fast a reaction happens depends on temperature. Almost all chemical reactions go faster when the temperature is higher. The higher the temperature at which we cook our food, the faster it cooks. Separating dirt from clothes is also a chemical process, and it too goes better in hot water. Chemists often use heat in the laboratory to make reactions take place more rapidly.

Energy and chemical change

The scientific idea of energy can explain a great deal about chemical reactions. In general, the energy that an object has is a measure of its ability to make things happen. For example, a fast-moving ball can break a pane of glass, make a hole in the ground, or knock over a group of pins in a bowling alley. The ball has energy to do these things because it is moving, and it gives up some of its energy of movement when it makes something happen. This type of energy is called kinetic energy, from the Greek word *kinesis* meaning "movement."

Another example is a lightbulb giving out energy in the form of light and heat. This energy comes from the electric current that flows through the lightbulb. The light makes light-sensitive cells in our eyes react, and this starts the process of seeing. The lightbulb also gives out invisible heat radiation, which warms objects nearby.

When iron is exposed to water and air for some time, it rusts. A brown iron compound is formed in this reaction.

21

ENERGY IN CHEMICAL REACTIONS

> **SCIENCE WORDS**
>
> - **Energy:** The ability to cause a change in something by heating it up, altering its shape, or making it move.
> - **Kinetic energy:** The energy of movement.
> - **Kinetic theory:** The study of heat flow and other processes in terms of the motion of the atoms and molecules involved.
> - **Molecule:** The smallest particle of a chemical substance that can exist on its own. Molecules consist of atoms bonded together.

In a chemical reaction, the energy in the substances is part of what makes the reaction happen. It also influences how the reaction happens.

Matter on the small scale

In explaining chemical change, chemists use their knowledge of how tiny atoms behave. All matter is made of atoms, and these often form groups bonded together, called molecules. Most—but not all—molecules are minutely small.

In the air around us, molecules of nitrogen and oxygen (the two main gases in the air) are pairs of atoms—although some oxygen exists as ozone, with three atoms. Carbon dioxide consists of one carbon atom linked to two oxygen atoms, while some other gases, such as argon and krypton, consist of single atoms only.

Groups of atoms may break up during chemical reactions, or at very high pressures and temperatures. For example, some molecules in the atmosphere are broken up into their atoms in the intense heat of a lightning discharge. The separate atoms that are produced soon react together and recombine to form the same molecules again.

Molecules in movement

Molecules are always moving. In a solid such as a rock, each molecule is constantly vibrating. However, the molecules do not move away from their "home" position, so the solid material does not easily change its size and shape. A rock does not change its shape if you push it with a finger (but if you hit the rock with a hammer it may break up).

In liquids, the molecules also vibrate, but they have more freedom to move around than the molecules in a solid. However, they are packed quite close together (as in a solid), and they also tend to stay in contact with neighboring molecules. The molecules move around in a loose group, passing each other and sliding past other molecules in the liquid. This is why liquid moves around in its container; juice, for example, takes the shape of the cup, jug, or whatever container it is poured into.

In a gas, the molecules are far apart and can fly around. They collide with each other and bounce off the walls of the container. The molecules not only move around, but also rotate and vibrate.

In air at normal temperatures—that is, about 68°F (20°C)—most of the molecules of oxygen and nitrogen move at approximately 1,500 feet per second (450 m/s),

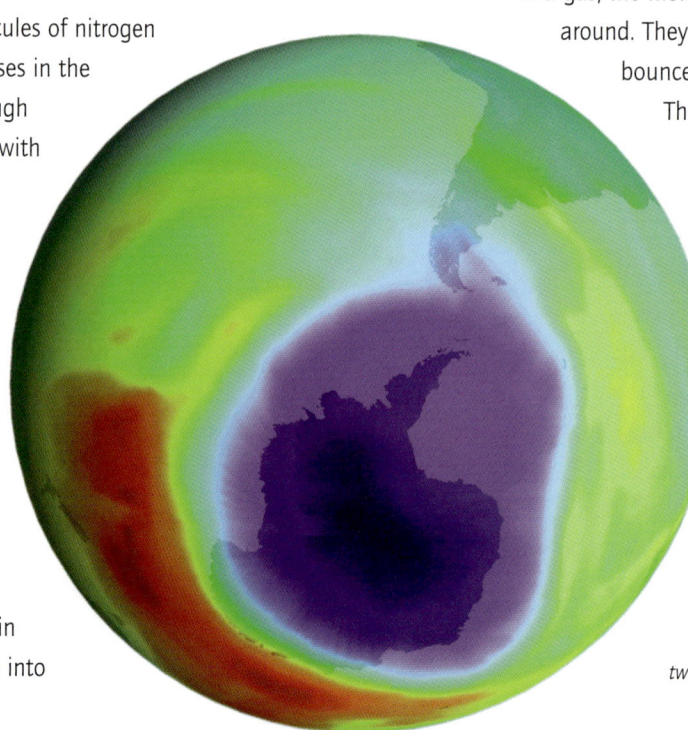

The depleted ozone layer over Antarctica is shaded purple. Ozone (O_3) molecules consist of three oxygen atoms, which break down to form normal two-atom molecules.

CHEMICAL REACTIONS

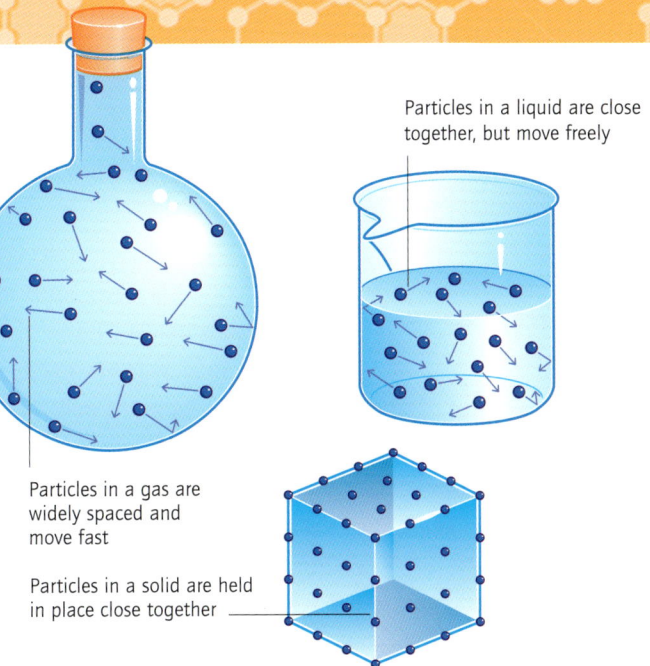

In the three main states of matter, the particles have different spacings and varying amounts of movement.

which is faster than the speed of sound. At any given moment, some molecules are traveling much faster than this, and some are moving much more slowly.

The idea that matter consists of myriad tiny particles in motion is called the kinetic theory of matter. In everyday speech, the word "theory" is sometimes used to mean an idea that has not been tried in practice. However, in science it means something quite different. A theory is a wide-ranging and detailed description that closely matches the known facts. There is nothing uncertain about the kinetic theory; it is well confirmed by a great many experiments over many years.

The gas laws

The kinetic theory assumes that gas molecules are like tiny balls, bouncing around inside a container. This idea gave the theory its first success by explaining many aspects of how gases behave.

First, when a molecule hits a wall of the container, it bounces back with unchanged speed and unchanged kinetic energy. At the same time, it pushes against the wall. This push is the pressure that we know a gas exerts on its container.

SIZES OF MOLECULES

Molecules can vary greatly in size. Most are tiny and are made up of just a few atoms. But some molecules in living things are much, much bigger. A single molecule of deoxyribonucleic acid (DNA) or ribonucleic acid (RNA)—the genetic materials found in the centers of cells—can consist of millions of atoms. Stretched out, a molecule of DNA from a human cell would be about 2 inches (5 cm) long! Many protein molecules are also large, containing hundreds of atoms. A single crystal of ordinary salt, sodium chloride, can also be regarded as one huge molecule. Its atoms do not form small groups, but instead link with their neighbors to form a huge, regularly spaced network of atoms called a crystal lattice.

Molecular model of an enzyme from the bacterium Helicobacter pylori, *a bacteria strongly linked to the development of gastric ulcers and stomach cancer.*

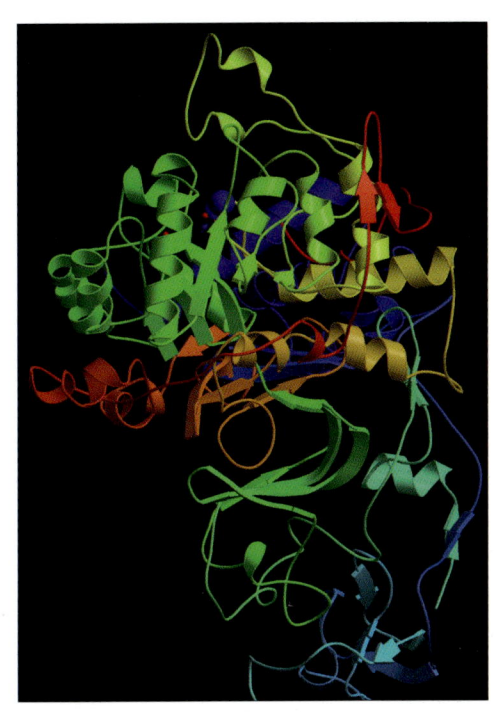

ENERGY IN CHEMICAL REACTIONS

Also, if the gas is squeezed into a smaller space, the molecules bounce off the walls more often, because they take less time moving from one wall to another. That explains why, as the gas is compressed and its volume decreases, the pressure increases.

If the molecules of a gas are speeded up, the pressure increases because the molecules exert a greater force on the walls when they bounce off them. The kinetic theory tells us that the average speed of the molecules increases as the temperature of the gas increases. That is why the pressure of a gas increases with temperature.

These relationships between volume, temperature, and pressure in a gas are called the gas laws. In fact, these laws only hold perfectly true for an "ideal" gas, which has these characteristics:

• The volume of the molecules is so small compared with the space around them that it can be ignored.

• When the molecules collide with the walls of the container they bounce off without losing any energy, so the total kinetic energy of the gas never decreases.

• The molecules are not attracted to each other or to the container walls.

In practice, the gas laws also apply to real gases, because they behave very similarly to ideal gases over a wide range of temperatures and pressures. As well as explaining how gases behave, the idea of moving molecules also explains a great deal about solids and liquids, and about chemical reactions.

Temperature and heat

The constant motion of molecules is what we know as temperature. The hotter a piece of matter is, the faster its molecules move. As matter cools, its molecules move more and more slowly.

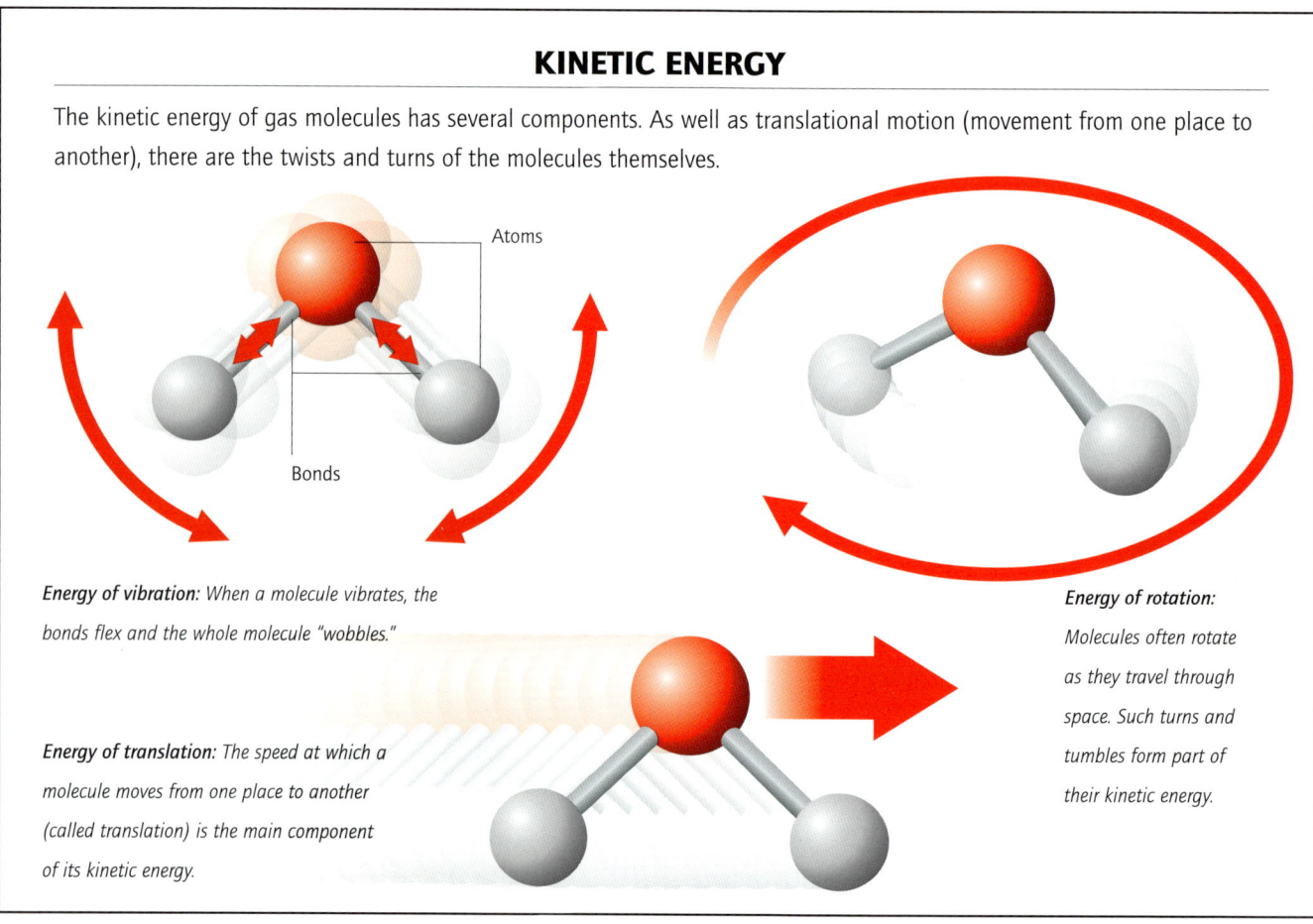

KINETIC ENERGY

The kinetic energy of gas molecules has several components. As well as translational motion (movement from one place to another), there are the twists and turns of the molecules themselves.

Energy of vibration: When a molecule vibrates, the bonds flex and the whole molecule "wobbles."

Energy of translation: The speed at which a molecule moves from one place to another (called translation) is the main component of its kinetic energy.

Energy of rotation: Molecules often rotate as they travel through space. Such turns and tumbles form part of their kinetic energy.

CHEMICAL REACTIONS

Biological samples can be quickly cooled to very low temperatures by immersing them in liquid nitrogen, which has a temperature of around –328°F (–200°C).

When two objects at different temperatures are in contact, the warmer one cools down and the cooler one warms up. So the molecules in the cooler object will start to move faster, and those in the warmer object will slow down. Kinetic energy is transferred from the faster-moving molecules of the hotter object to the slower-moving molecules of the cooler one.

This transfer of kinetic energy is called a flow of heat. A flow of heat is not only caused by a change in temperature, but it also produces a change in temperature (the hot object gets cooler and the cool object gets warmer). However, as we know from the gas laws, heat flow can also cause other sorts of changes. For example, if gas in a closed container is heated, the gas will get warmer and its pressure will also increase. But if the gas is free to expand outside the container, heating will cause expansion rather than increase the pressure. So heat can make a gas expand or increase its pressure, as well as raise its temperature.

A flow of heat can also cause matter to change its state—that is, whether it is a solid, liquid, or a gas. When an ice cube floating in a glass of warm soda melts, heat flows into the ice from the soda. While the ice is still below its melting point of 32°F (0°C), the heat warms the ice up. When the ice reaches its melting point, it begins to turn into water. As the ice is melting, its temperature stays at 32°F (0°C). At this point, the flow of heat is causing a change of state from solid to liquid, not a temperature change. Similarly, when water is boiled, heat flows into it, turning it into steam. The liquid water and the steam stay at the same temperature, 212°F (100°C), until all the water has been turned into steam.

Bonds and chemical energy

Matter contains energy because its molecules are moving, and because of the way in which the atoms that make up its molecules are joined.

When atoms link together in a chemical reaction, they are said to form chemical bonds. These bonds, or

Pioneers of Kinetic Theory

The great 17th-century English scientist Isaac Newton (1642–1727) believed that gases behave the way they do because their particles repel each other (push each other apart), even when they are not in contact. In 1738, the Dutch-born Swiss scientist Daniel Bernoulli (1700–1782) instead suggested—correctly—that the pressure of gases is due only to the collisions of their particles with the walls of the container. This important idea was largely ignored until English scientist John Herapath (1790–1868) revived it. Even then, scientists generally did not accept the kinetic theory until the experiments of English physicist James Prescott Joule (1818–1889) and the detailed mathematical work of Scottish physicist James Clerk Maxwell (1831–1879) finally proved it beyond all doubt.

ENERGY IN CHEMICAL REACTIONS

links, can be strong or weak, and there can be more than one bond between two atoms.

It takes energy to break a chemical bond, because energy must be put in in order to pull the atoms apart. The atoms can either be heated, or alternatively another atom can come into contact with them, forming new bonds as the old ones break. Once the atoms are separated, they still have this energy. So, if the atoms recombine and the bonds are re-formed, they give out the energy.

So forming chemical bonds means energy is given out, and breaking chemical bonds means energy must be put in. During chemical reactions, energy is taken in as bonds break and given out as bonds form. When a flask is heated in the laboratory to make a reaction happen, energy is taken in. Energy can also be taken in from radiation. For example, the chemicals in photographic film take in energy when exposed to light, which is a form of radiation. The chemicals react, producing a photographic image after the film has been chemically processed.

> ### SCIENCE WORDS
>
> - **Bond:** A chemical link between atoms.
> - **Endothermic reaction:** One in which the reacting substances take in heat.
> - **Exothermic reaction:** One in which the reacting substances give out heat.
> - **Heat energy:** Energy that flows as a result of a temperature difference.
> - **Products:** The substances produced in a chemical reaction.
> - **Reactants:** The substances that react together in a chemical reaction.
> - **State of matter:** One of the forms that a substance can take, depending on its temperature and pressure.
> - **Thermodynamics:** The study of how heat and other forms of energy are converted.

Corn uses energy from sunlight to build molecules of the sugar glucose from water and carbon dioxide. This endothermic reaction could not happen without the plant's complex chemical apparatus.

Exothermic and endothermic reactions

Chemical reactions that give out energy are called exothermic. The word comes from the Greek words *exo* meaning "outside" and *therme* meaning "heat." However, the energy given out can be in the form not only of heat, but also in the form of light, sound, movement, an electric current, and so on.

The burning of gas or wood is an exothermic reaction. Some of the heat given out travels away from the fire as heat radiation, and some of it goes into the ash, smoke, and gas produced. Some heat also goes into the unburned fuel, which keeps the reaction going (as it needs a high temperature to proceed).

Likewise, reactions that take in energy are called endothermic, from the Greek words *endo* meaning "inside" and *therme* meaning "heat." When they are growing, plants absorb the energy of sunlight to build up their tissues. This process, which is called photosynthesis,

CHEMICAL REACTIONS

MEASURING TEMPERATURE

Chemists and other scientists need to measure temperature accurately. To do this, they use thermometers. One familiar type of thermometer uses a thin column of liquid mercury (or alcohol) inside a glass tube. The mercury expands when it gets warmer, and the end of the column moves along the tube, which is marked in units of temperature. Temperature can also be measured by its effect on electrical circuits. A current generally flows in a wire more easily if the temperature of the wire is lower, and so measuring the resistance of a wire can provide a way of measuring temperature. Instruments called thermocouples also use wires to measure temperature. Because thermocouples are cheap and more robust than glass thermometers, they are often very convenient to use. Another device called a pyrometer uses the fact that very hot materials give out light of a characteristic color—for example, the glow of red-hot iron. Analyzing the color of light from a hot object can be used to reveal its temperature.

Many different instruments are used to measure temperature. Glass thermometers were traditionally most used, but electronic versions are now replacing these. Pyrometers use the light from hot, glowing objects to find temperatures. A measured current through a wire is adjusted until the wire's color matches that of the hot object.

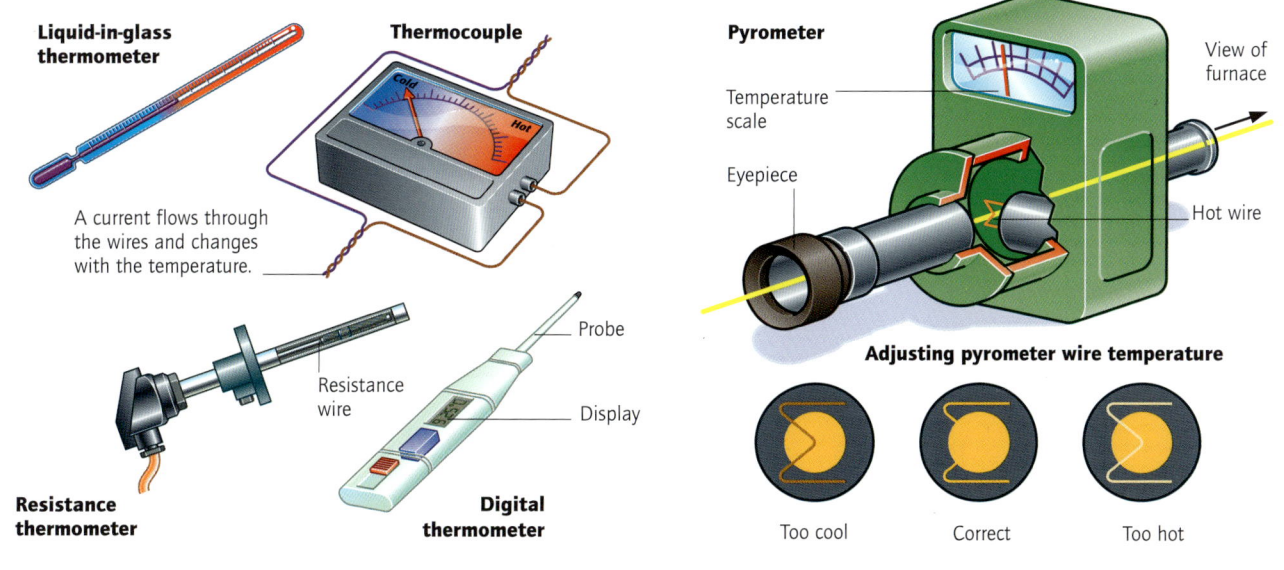

is endothermic. Another endothermic reaction is the breakdown of calcium carbonate (limestone) into lime (calcium oxide) and carbon dioxide. This reaction needs a supply of heat to provide the energy required.

Thermodynamics: the first law

One of the most fundamental laws in the whole of science is the law of conservation of energy. It states that, in any chemical or physical process, the total energy of everything involved is the same afterward as it was before. This means that, in a chemical reaction, the total sum of the kinetic energies of molecules, the energies of chemical bonds, and the energies of heat and light involved must be exactly the same after the reaction has taken place as they were before it.

The law of conservation of energy is basic to the science of thermodynamics, which deals with the relationships between heat and other forms of energy. That is why the law of conservation of energy is often called the first law of thermodynamics.

HEAT AND CHEMICAL REACTIONS

Substances change during chemical reactions, and so does the amount of energy they store. These changes provide the energy that is given out in reactions.

Chemists often need to study the heat taken in or given out in chemical reactions. The amount of heat taken in or given out is called the heat of reaction. To measure heats of reaction, people use devices called calorimeters.

Measuring heats of reaction

There are various types of calorimeters. One type is called a bomb calorimeter, because the reaction takes place inside a strong casing like that around a bomb. The casing must be able to withstand the high pressures that sometimes develop during a reaction. This casing is surrounded by water. The reaction that takes place inside either gives out heat, warming the water, or it takes in heat from the water, cooling it down. The experimenter measures the temperature of the water before and after the reaction takes place. From the temperature change, the amount of heat that has flowed in or out is calculated: the greater the change, the greater is the heat of reaction.

Another type of calorimeter, called a flame calorimeter, can be used for reactions that involve burning. Other types of calorimeters can be used for other types of reactions—for example, mixing an acid and a base so that they neutralize each other.

The labels on food packaging provide information on calorific values—that is, how much energy the food will yield when it is used in chemical reactions in the body.

Heat, energy, and expansion

Imagine a reaction taking place in a closed container (such as a calorimeter), so that the volume of all the reactants is constant. The reaction gives out gas as a product, together with energy. Some of the energy is in the form of heat, so the reaction products increase in temperature. The rest of the energy produced is stored in the chemical bonds of the products.

If the same reaction takes place instead in an open container, the products will heat up slightly less than in the closed container. So, what has happened to the energy that has "disappeared?" The gas produced has expanded, pushing against the pressure of the surrounding air and using up energy as it does so. Less energy therefore remains to be turned

CHEMICAL REACTIONS

We obtain energy from the food we eat. The more calories a food has, the more energy it produces. Chocolate cakes contain many calories.

into heat. As the heated gases expand and push back the air, they give a little bit of energy to the air molecules, so no energy has been lost. (The solids and liquids involved change volume by only a tiny amount compared with the gases, so the energy they lose through expansion would not be noticeable.)

Doing work

When heated gases expand, they do what scientists call work. Work is done whenever a force moves something. The amount of work is defined as the force multiplied by the distance moved in the direction of the force. So, suppose you lift a heavy book off the floor onto a desk. You apply a force to lift the book (against the force of gravity) through the distance from the floor to the desktop. The energy to do this work was provided by chemical reactions in your muscles.

USING A BOMB CALORIMETER

In a bomb calorimeter, a substance is burned in oxygen to find out how much heat is given out. The substance is weighed and placed in the "bomb," and oxygen is pumped in under pressure. The reaction is started by an electrical spark. A stirrer is used to equalize the temperature throughout the water, while the insulated walls of the calorimeter prevent heat from escaping. The change in the water's temperature is measured using a thermometer.

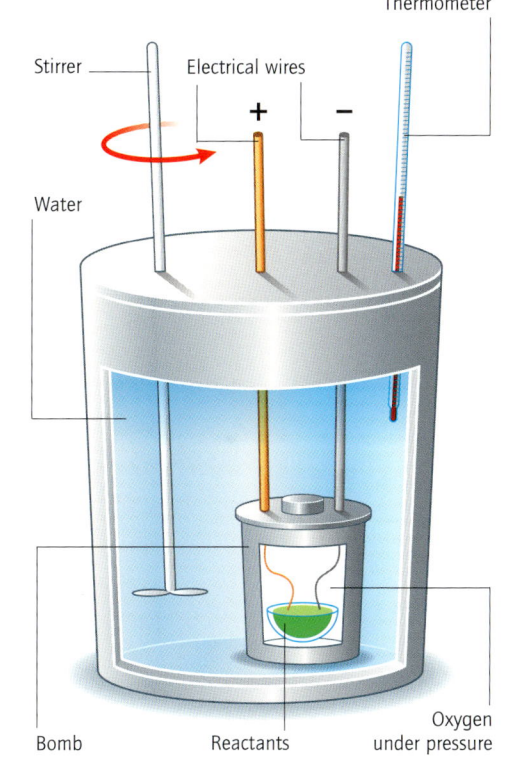

HEAT AND CHEMICAL REACTIONS

THE COFFEE-CUP CALORIMETER

A simple calorimeter for heat experiments can be made from two expanded polystyrene cups nested together, with a lid. Expanded polystyrene is a good heat insulator (heat does not easily flow through it), which is why cups made of this material are good for keeping coffee hot or soda cold. The experimenter places the experimental substances in the cups and mixes them together. These could be weighed quantities of reactants, or a solid and a liquid at different temperatures, depending on the experiment. He or she then reads the temperature using the thermometer pushed through the lid.

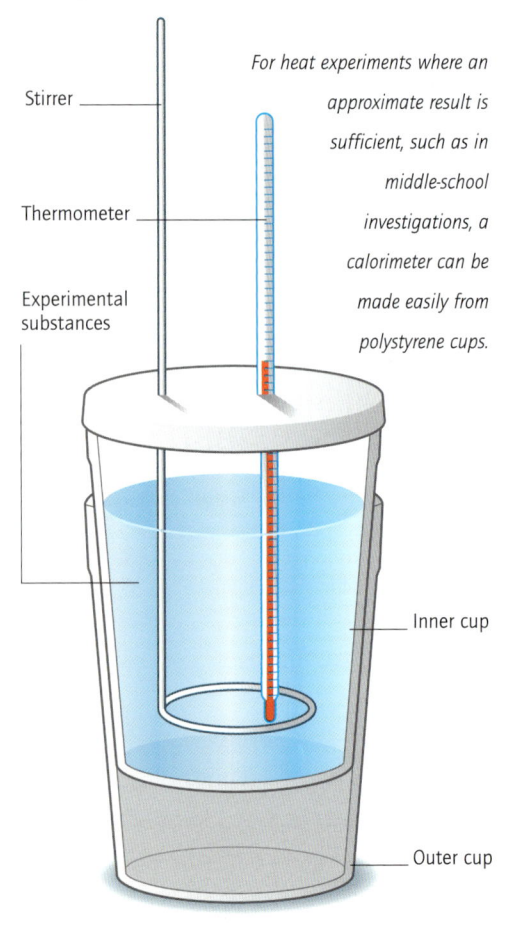

For heat experiments where an approximate result is sufficient, such as in middle-school investigations, a calorimeter can be made easily from polystyrene cups.

Stirrer
Thermometer
Experimental substances
Inner cup
Outer cup

Some chemical energy in your body has been used up in doing work.

Work can be done in producing other kinds of energy. When you roll a bowling ball, the force of your hand moves the ball through a certain distance before you let it go. Your body does work, and gives the ball kinetic energy.

Potential energy

Kinetic energy is one form of energy and heat is another form. There is also another form of energy called potential energy. Things have potential energy because of their position or the arrangement of their parts. When you lift a book onto a desk, you give it potential energy. (In fact, the potential energy gained is equal to the work done in lifting the book.) Potential

CHEMICAL REACTIONS

energy can be converted into other forms of energy; for example, if the book were to fall off the desk, some of the potential energy would be converted into kinetic energy (energy of motion). A stretched spring also has potential energy: when released, it jumps back to its original length and the potential energy is converted into kinetic energy.

Chemical energy is also a kind of potential energy. The energy stored in chemical bonds can be converted into heat, light, sound, or motion when a chemical reaction takes place. Another important type of potential energy is electrical potential energy, which makes an electric current flow.

When we bowl or throw a ball, chemical reactions in our muscles convert energy stored in the body into energy of movement.

> ### SCIENCE WORDS
> - **Calorimeter:** Apparatus for accurately measuring heat given out or taken in.
> - **Heat capacity:** The amount of heat required to change the temperature of an object by 1°C (1.8°F).
> - **Specific heat capacity:** The amount of heat required to change the temperature of a specified amount of a substance by 1°C (1.8°F).

In many processes, potential energy decreases as it is converted into other sorts of energy. As a general rule, systems tend to lose potential energy. For example, when an oil drum lying at the top of a hill rolls down the hill, it has less potential energy at the bottom of the hill than it does at the top. Similarly, a chemical reaction is likely to happen if the products have less chemical energy than the reactants.

Rusting is a reaction that releases a lot of energy. The reaction product is hydrated iron oxide, made up of iron, oxygen, and water. This has much less energy than the reactants that go into it. Although the rusting process gives out energy and needs no heat to begin, it

HEAT CAPACITY

To calculate the heat given out or taken in by a reaction, chemists need to know how much heat the calorimeter itself gives out or takes in. This means the experimenter first needs to find out what the "heat capacity" of the calorimeter is. The heat capacity of an object is the amount of heat needed to change its temperature by 1 degree Celsius (1°C, 1.8°F). The calorimeter's heat capacity is multiplied by the temperature change in the experiment to give the amount of heat flowing into or out of the apparatus.

HEAT AND CHEMICAL REACTIONS

TRY THIS

Comparing heat loss

For this experiment, use hot water from the faucet. (This is hot enough: do not use boiling water.) First, warm a vacuum flask and a jug by filling both with hot water and leaving for a few minutes. Then pour out the water.

Next, fill the vacuum flask, pour that water into the jug and put the lid on. Refill the vacuum flask and put its cap on tightly. This ensures the jug contains the same amount of water as the flask, so that you can make a fair comparison between them.

Measure and write down the temperature of the water in the two containers after 20 minutes, 40 minutes, and 1 hour. Each time you measure the temperature, keep the thermometer in the water for 30 seconds to give the thermometer time to come to the right temperature. Quickly re-stopper the flask and cover the jug after each temperature measurement.

Label your tables of measurements "isolated system" for the flask and "closed system" for the jug. You can also plot

Measure the temperature of the water in both the jug and flask at regular intervals using a thermometer.

The jug should be filled using the vacuum flask. That way the flask and the jug will contain the same amount of water.

graphs of the temperatures against the time passed. Finally, repeat the experiment with the jug, again filling it from the vacuum flask. This time, leave the lid off the jug. Label these results "open system." Again, you can plot the results on a graph.

You should have found that the system that lost heat fastest was the jug without a lid. This is an open system: it can exchange energy and matter with its surroundings. Some of the water molecules escaped into the air, taking heat energy with them.

The jug with a lid on is a closed system; the hot water all stayed inside. It should have lost heat not as fast as the open jug. The vacuum flask is close to being an isolated system. It is designed to lose heat only very slowly, and its tight stopper prevents water vapor from being lost. You should have found that its temperature went down by the smallest amount over the times measured.

CHEMICAL REACTIONS

CAR BATTERIES

Electrical energy can flow in or out of the substances involved in a chemical reaction; chemical reactions can release this energy or store it up. When a car is at rest, the car battery uses chemical reactions to deliver electrical energy to the lights and the radio, where it is converted into light and sound. When the car is moving, a generator connected to the engine drives an electric current through the battery in the opposite direction. This reverses the chemical reactions in the battery and stores energy for later use.

Cars have rechargeable batteries. Energy used to power the lights and radio when the car is at rest is replaced once the car is moving.

occurs only slowly. Comparing it with the oil drum rolling downhill, it is as if the oil drum were rolling through mud.

Making reactions happen

Even if a mixture of chemical substances can lose energy by changing in some process, that process may not happen unaided. In the same way, if an oil drum at the top of the hill is standing upright, it will need to be toppled over to start it rolling. If it is on its side but is lying in a shallow hole, it will need a shove to lift it out of the hole and start it moving.

Burning paper is another chemical reaction that, like rusting, releases a great deal of energy. Again, the energy of the products is less than that of the reactants, with the energy difference given out as heat. But the paper does not burst into flame spontaneously (by itself). It needs some help from a lighted match or another source of heat to start it off. This is rather like an oil drum lying in a hollow, which needs a jolt to get it going.

Energy-absorbing reactions

Chemical reactions in which the products have higher energy than the reactants have to take in energy to go ahead. The cold packs found in first-aid kits use reactions like this. When the pack is used, it rapidly becomes very cold and can be pressed against wounds to ease pain and reduce swellings. One type of cold pack consists of a strong outer bag containing

The elastic band in this catapult stores potential energy when it is pulled tight. When let go, this turns into kinetic energy, sending an object flying.

HEAT AND CHEMICAL REACTIONS

ELECTROMAGNETIC RADIATION

Energy can enter or leave a chemical reaction as radiation in various forms. Light and heat radiation form part of the electromagnetic spectrum—a vastly extended version of the visible light spectrum, which is the array of colors that we see in a rainbow. The electromagnetic spectrum includes all the different forms of electromagnetic radiation arranged according to their wavelength (the distance from one wave's peak or trough to the next wave's peak or trough). At one end, there are radio waves, which can have wavelengths more than 1 mile (1.5 km) long; at the other end, are gamma rays—very high-energy waves given out in nuclear reactions. The main types of electromagnetic radiation that are important in chemical reactions are:

- Visible light, which is given out in many chemical reactions including exploding fireworks. The light given off by glowworms and fireflies also comes from chemical reactions in their bodies. Light can cause chemical reactions, as well as be emitted in reactions.

- Infrared radiation ("heat radiation"), which has longer wavelengths than visible light and, like light, can travel through space (unlike other forms of heating).

- Ultraviolet radiation, which has shorter wavelengths than visible light and which causes the burning and tanning reactions in our skin.

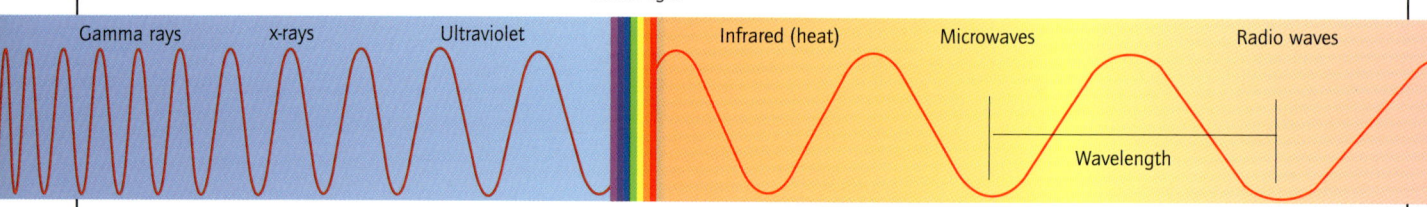

In the electromagnetic spectrum, gamma rays have the highest energies and shortest wavelengths (about a hundred billionths of a millimeter long). Radio waves have wavelengths about a hundred million million times larger.

powdered ammonium nitrate and an inner bag made of a weaker plastic and containing water. If the outer bag is struck or squeezed hard, the inner bag bursts and the water and ammonium nitrate mix. The ammonium nitrate dissolves in the water, absorbing heat so strongly that the temperature of the liquid can drop to 32°F (0°C).

In this endothermic reaction, the products of the dissolving process have higher energy in their chemical bonds than the reactants. The extra energy is taken in from the reactants and their surroundings, lowering

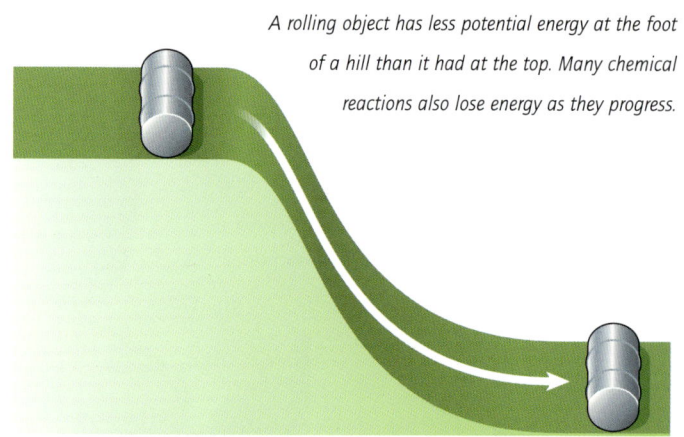

A rolling object has less potential energy at the foot of a hill than it had at the top. Many chemical reactions also lose energy as they progress.

CHEMICAL REACTIONS

their temperature. Although the products have gained energy compared with the reactants, no energy has been created or destroyed overall. The total amount of energy stays the same, in line with the first law of thermodynamics. The energy taken in from the surroundings is stored in the products as chemical energy within the bonds.

Internal energy and enthalpy

The total energy within a piece of matter is called its internal energy. This is made up of the total kinetic energy of all the particles in the matter (due to their movements), plus the potential energy stored in the chemical bonds of the substances that make it up. If heat is given out or taken in during a reaction, the internal energy of the substances will decrease or increase accordingly.

Chemists use the term enthalpy change for changes in internal energy that take place during reactions. If the pressure is constant (such as when the reaction takes place at normal air pressure), the enthalpy change in a reaction is equal to the change in internal energy between the reactants and the products. Enthalpy is measured in the same units as energy joules or calories. If a reaction is exothermic (that is, energy is given out), the enthalpy change is a negative amount, because the energy of the products is less than that of the reactants. Similarly, for endothermic reactions, enthalpy changes are positive. For example,

> **SCIENCE WORDS**
>
> - **Electromagnetic radiation:** Radiation forming part of the electromagnetic spectrum, such as light, heat radiation, and ultraviolet (UV) light.
> - **Enthalpy change:** At constant pressure, the change in internal energy that occurs during any process.
> - **Internal energy:** The total kinetic energy of all the particles in a system, plus all the chemical energy.
> - **Potential energy:** Energy that something has because of the way it is positioned or how its parts are arranged.
> - **Spontaneous reaction:** A reaction that happens by itself, without needing something from outside to start it off.
> - **Wavelength:** The distance measured from the peak or trough of one wave to the peak or trough of the next.

the enthalpy change when 1 gram of water evaporates is 2.26 kilojoules (a kilojoule is 1,000 joules), or 9.46 kilocalories. The reverse process (when 1 gram of water condenses from gas to liquid) has an enthalpy change of minus 2.26 kilojoules (minus 9.46 kilocalories).

Hess's law

Hess's law was formulated by Russian chemist Germain Henri Hess (1802–1850). The law states that the overall enthalpy change that accompanies a chemical reaction is independent of the route by which the reaction takes place. So, for example, if substance A can be converted into substance B by two different chemical processes, the total energy changes in each process must add up to the same amount. Hess's law is a version of the law of conservation of energy (or the first law of thermodynamics), since otherwise energy would need to be created or destroyed along the way.

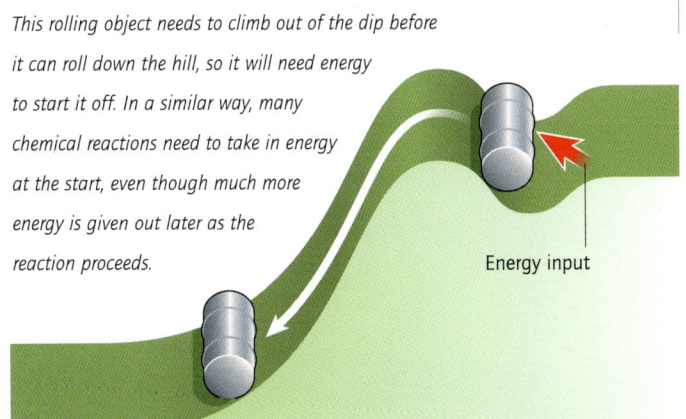

This rolling object needs to climb out of the dip before it can roll down the hill, so it will need energy to start it off. In a similar way, many chemical reactions need to take in energy at the start, even though much more energy is given out later as the reaction proceeds.

Energy input

ENTROPY AND FREE ENERGY

Energy drives reactions, but so does another factor called entropy. Although we are normally unaware of entropy, it also plays a part in everyday life.

What causes some chemical reactions to occur spontaneously (by themselves)? We have seen in the previous chapter that many reactions give out energy, but not all; and not all reactions that give out energy happen spontaneously. To explain which reactions occur and which do not, we need to look at another factor that is at work alongside energy, acting as a driving force in reactions. This important factor is called entropy.

Entropy

Entropy is related to disorder. To get an idea of what entropy is, imagine a gas-tight container is divided into halves by a partition, and that one half (compartment A) contains gas at ordinary atmospheric pressure, while the other half (compartment B) is completely empty. If a door in the partition is opened, what will happen?

We would expect the gas instantly to begin diffusing (spreading) from compartment A into compartment B. It will continue to do so until the gas fills the two halves of the container at equal pressure. In the same way, we do not expect all the air in a room occasionally to clump together in one corner and stay there.

After the door in the central partition is opened, all molecules of the gas could wander into one half of the container or the other, just by chance. That would not violate any physical laws, such as the law of conservation of energy. It is simply very, very unlikely. Since the molecules are in constant movement, it is likely that the molecules will fill the space in the course of their wanderings. If instead, we found gas crowding into one part of the container, we would think that some force was organizing the molecules. (Just as, if we saw people in a park gathering in one place, we would think something was happening to draw them to that area.)

Having all the molecules crowded together in one part of the available space is described as the gas being in an organized state. When they are spread out evenly through the available space, that is described as a disorganized state—or a "nothing special" state.

Entropy is a measure of disorder, so the entropy of the spread-out, disorganized gas is much higher than that of the crowded-together gas. The gas naturally tends to go from the highly organized state to the less organized state, so its entropy tends to increase. We find this too in everyday life. Shoelaces often come undone, but they never tie themselves into neat bows. It takes a special effort to tidy a bedroom, but not to make it untidy. So, unlike with energy, the total entropy of the universe generally increases all the time (although in particular locations it may decrease for a while).

Entropy is the driving force that makes evaporation happen, forming the mist in this lake landscape.

CHEMICAL REACTIONS

Entropy versus energy

Entropy increases in many processes. When a liquid evaporates, its molecules leave the liquid to move about in the space above it. They are less organized than when they were confined to the liquid, so the system's entropy increases.

When they are in the liquid, the molecules stay together because they attract each other. When a molecule leaves the liquid, each molecule does work by moving against these forces. The molecules therefore need energy to evaporate. They take this energy from the liquid, cooling it down.

In some chemical reactions, there is more gas in the products formed than in the initial reactants (for example, when a solid and liquid are mixed and a gas is produced.) In these reactions, the entropy almost always increases. The disorder of molecules when they are spread out within a gas is far greater than when they are confined to the much smaller volume of a solid or liquid.

ENTROPY IN ACTION

Two different gases are separately stored in a container (1). When the partition is taken away (2), the gases begin to diffuse into each other's space and entropy increases. Eventually, the gases become more evenly mixed throughout (3).

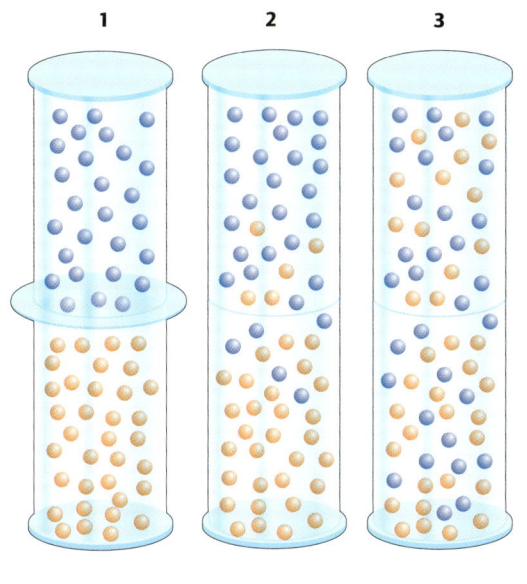

Gibbs free energy

The ideas of energy and entropy can be put together to understand exactly why some reactions happen spontaneously and others do not. But one extra idea is needed: that of Gibbs free energy, named for the U.S. scientist Willard Gibbs (1839–1903). Gibbs discovered an equation that used the changes in enthalpy and entropy in a reaction to predict whether the reaction would occur. This equation makes the following statement:

Change in Gibbs free energy =
(change in enthalpy) −
(temperature x change in entropy)

In other words, the change in entropy (multiplied by the temperature) has to be taken away from the

37

ENTROPY AND FREE ENERGY

TRY THIS

The odds against it

To get a "feel" for entropy, you can try calculating the probability of a small number of gas molecules all crowding into one half of a container divided into two compartments, A and B.

To make this simpler, imagine there are only four molecules in the container instead of the vast number that there really would be. If you checked their positions at a given moment, you might find three molecules in A and one in B, which you could write as AAAB; or you might find the first and third molecules in A and the second and fourth in B, which you could write as ABAB; and so on. These are different "microstates" of the gas.

First, write down all the possible microstates of the four molecules in the two compartments.

You should find 16 microstates in all. These are: AAAA, AAAB, AABA, AABB, ABAA, ABAB, ABBA, ABBB, BAAA, BAAB, BABA, BABB, BBAA, BBAB, BBBA, and BBBB.

Now count up, from among these 16 microstates:
• The number of microstates in which all molecules are in one compartment, A or B.
• The number of microstates in which there are equal numbers of molecules in both compartments.
• The number of microstates in which there are three molecules in one compartment and one molecule in the other compartment.

You should find that there is one microstate (AAAA) in which all the molecules are in A and one (BBBB) in which they are all in B. So there are 2 chances in 16, or 1 in 8, of all the molecules of the gas being in one compartment at any moment.

There are eight microstates in which there are three molecules in one compartment and one in the other; and six microstates in which there are two molecules in each compartment. Adding these together gives 14 microstates (out of a total of 16) in which, at a given moment, the molecules are roughly evenly divided between the two compartments. That is a probability of 7 in 8—much higher than the 1 in 8 probability of all the molecules being in one compartment.

So, even for a very few molecules, finding the gas squeezed into one compartment is unlikely. The same thing holds true even more strongly for real gases, where there are trillions and trillions of molecules in even a tiny volume. Then, it is overwhelmingly likely that the gas will spread evenly through the available space.

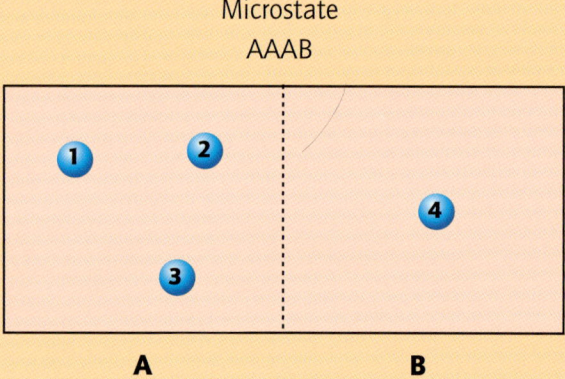

Microstate AAAB

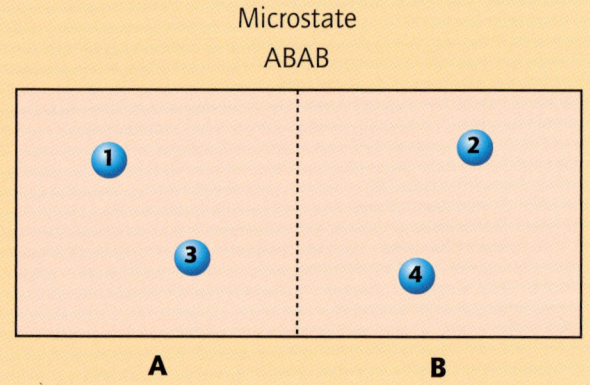

Microstate ABAB

CHEMICAL REACTIONS

Solid sodium chloride (common salt)

Sodium ion (Na^+)
Chloride ion (Cl^-)

Water (H_2O)

Dissolved sodium chloride

When a solid such as sodium chloride (salt) dissolves in a liquid, its entropy increases because of the greater disorder of particles within a liquid.

enthalpy change in the reaction to give the change in Gibbs free energy. This is very important, because it is only when the Gibbs free energy decreases (that is, the change in Gibbs free energy is negative) that a reaction will take place spontaneously. So, if the change in entropy is large enough, it can produce a negative change in Gibbs free energy overall, even if the enthalpy change is positive (as in an endothermic reaction). That is why some reactions that take in energy do occur spontaneously.

For example, in dissolving, the increase in entropy produces a negative change in Gibbs free energy, even though energy is taken in. In this case, the driving force of the entropy increase wins out over the braking effect of the enthalpy increase. Similarly, an exothermic reaction that produces a decrease in entropy may not happen spontaneously because the decrease in entropy cancels out the negative enthalpy change.

The flow of heat

Heat diffuses (spreads) in much the same way that a gas does. If a hot body and a cold body come into contact, the molecular motions of the hot body spread to the molecules of the cooler body. This is because in a hot body, the average kinetic energy of the molecules is higher than in a cooler one. So when a molecule in the hot body collides with one in the cooler body, some kinetic energy will be passed from the hot body to the cooler one. In this way, kinetic energy is gradually passed from the hotter body to the cooler one, which amounts to a flow of heat in the same direction. A flow of heat in the other direction (from the cooler body to the hotter one) is not forbidden by the first law of thermodynamics, as energy would not be created or destroyed. However, it is fantastically improbable, just as gas molecules failing to spread out into an empty space is so unlikely.

The second law

An isolated system is one that cannot exchange matter or energy with its surroundings. The second law of thermodynamics states that, in an isolated system, entropy will increase or stay the same; it will never decrease.

A vacuum flask is close to being an isolated system (although it slowly loses heat energy to its surroundings). Imagine putting some hot water into the flask. At first, the water is hot and the flask itself is cooler, but then temperature differences start to disappear. The hot water cools a little as it warms the inner wall of the flask. Slight differences in temperature between the different parts of the liquid even out. As the temperature differences disappear, the

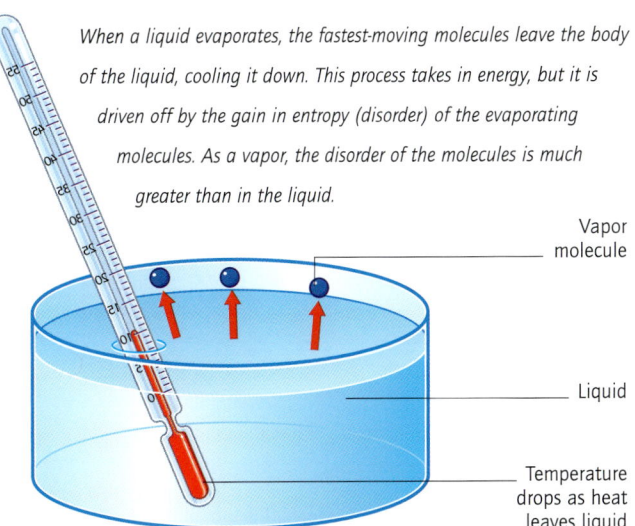

When a liquid evaporates, the fastest-moving molecules leave the body of the liquid, cooling it down. This process takes in energy, but it is driven off by the gain in entropy (disorder) of the evaporating molecules. As a vapor, the disorder of the molecules is much greater than in the liquid.

Vapor molecule

Liquid

Temperature drops as heat leaves liquid

ENTROPY AND FREE ENERGY

system becomes less organized. Eventually the liquid and the inner wall of the flask are at the same temperature and the system has maximum entropy.

On a very large scale, the second law of thermodynamics applies to the universe as a whole. For example, a cluster of stars, perhaps circled by planets, is a relatively low-entropy system, because it is highly ordered and organized compared with the mass of gas and dust from which it formed. But as the stars and planets developed, they gave out radiation energy. This spread out into space and warmed interstellar gas and dust. The increase in temperature raised the entropy in interstellar space, and increased the entropy of the universe itself.

Another form of the second law of thermodynamics refers to temperature rather than entropy. In this form, the law states that heat never flows by itself from a cooler body to a hotter body. If it seems to do so, something else is driving the process. (This form of the second law looks very different from the entropy version, but in thermodynamic terms it is exactly equivalent.)

For example, in a refrigerator, heat is continually removed from the cool interior. This heat flows out from cooling pipes behind the refrigerator into the room, which of course is warmer than the inside of the fridge. But this flow of heat from cool to warm is powered by the fridge's electric motor.

Entropy in open systems

Most real-life systems are open: they can exchange matter and energy with their surroundings. In an open system, entropy can decrease if the entropy of its surrounding increases at the same time.

For example, living things consist of structures that would be highly improbable if they came about by chance. Living things are, in fact, organized by the genes (units of inherited information) within cells. When an animal grows and develops, the process involves an enormous decrease in entropy. But this decrease is more than offset by the increase in entropy passing to the living creature's surroundings as it excretes waste matter and heat.

In a freezer, water is frozen and its entropy decreases as its molecules pass from the relatively disordered state of a liquid to the more ordered state of crystalline ice. But the entropy of the freezer plus its surroundings increases, because waste heat is pumped out of the back of the machine and increases the entropy of the air there. In a similar way, when water freezes spontaneously in cold weather, its own entropy decreases; however, the entropy of the water plus its surroundings increases, because of the heat given out in the freezing process.

Entropy and temperature

When heat flows in a system, there is almost always an increase in the entropy of the system, because heat is a disordering influence. The amount of entropy change is greater if the heat flow is greater. But the effect of heat in increasing disorder is also related to how orderly the system already is. The cooler something is, the more orderly it is, and the greater the amount of disorder that will be caused by a given amount of heat. So, for example, a given amount heat will cause

> ### SCIENCE WORDS
>
> - **Absolute zero:** The lowest theoretically possible temperature, –459.67°F (–273.15°C).
> - **Entropy:** A measure of the amount of disorder in any system.
> - **Gibbs free energy:** A decrease in Gibbs free energy means that a reaction will happen spontaneously.
> - **Kelvin scale:** Temperature scale that uses kelvins (K) as the unit of temperature, and where zero (0 K) is absolute zero (–459.67°F; –273.15°C).
> - **Microstate:** The state of a substance on the molecular scale—that is, the masses, speeds, and positions of all its molecules.

CHEMICAL REACTIONS

a greater entropy increase in a mass of ice than in an equal mass of steam.

Absolute zero

Most people are familiar with the Fahrenheit and the Celsius scales. Scientists, though, commonly use the Kelvin scale, with temperatures measured in kelvins (K), named for its inventor, the British scientist Lord Kelvin (1824–1907). This scale uses intervals of the same size as the Celsius (or centigrade) scale, where one degree is equal to one-hundredth of the difference between the temperature at which pure water boils and ice melts. (This is equal to nine-fifths of a degree on the Fahrenheit scale.) But on the Kelvin scale, zero is at

The average temperature in the universe is thought to be about 2.73K, or 2.73 degrees on the Kelvin scale (−454.76°F, −270.42°C). This is still a few degrees warmer than absolute zero.

"absolute zero." On this scale, water freezes at 273.15K and boils at 373.15K. But what exactly is absolute zero?

As an object is cooled, the movements of its molecules slow down. Eventually a point would be reached at which the movements are as slow as they can possibly be. This point, which is at the extremely cold temperature of −459.67°F (−273.15°C), is called absolute zero.

Scientists first put forward the concept of absolute zero from studying gases. When a gas is cooled, its pressure decreases. This process comes to an end when eventually the pressure would fall to zero for a theoretical ideal gas. This lowest possible temperature is absolute zero.

Although it is not possible to reach exactly absolute zero in practice, scientists have been able to cool matter to just a tiny fraction of a degree above this temperature. At these very low temperatures, matter starts behaving very oddly indeed.

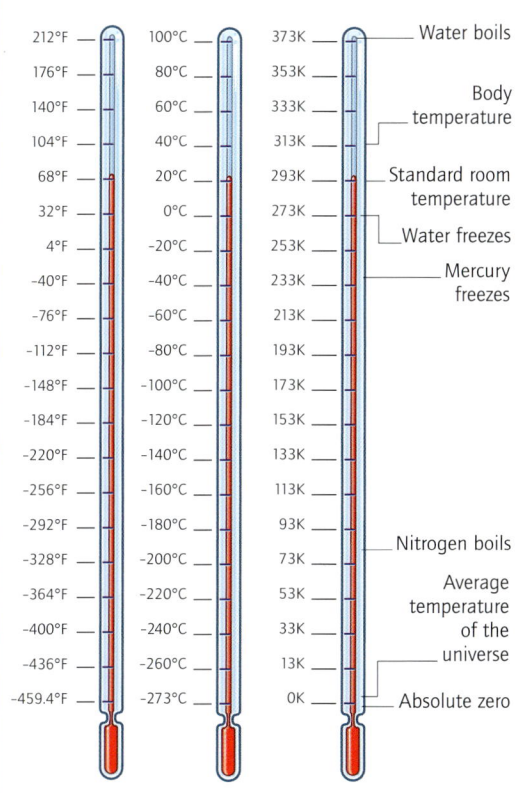

THREE SCALES

The Fahrenheit (°F), Celsius or centigrade (°C), and Kelvin (K) scales are the three temperature scales in common or scientific use.

RATES OF REACTIONS

How fast reactions happen depends on the substances involved, and also on other factors that can be controlled, such as temperature and concentration.

In all chemical reactions, bonds between atoms are broken and new bonds are made. For example, in the burning of methane (CH_4) in oxygen (O_2), the bonds between the carbon, hydrogen, and oxygen atoms are all broken and new links are formed:

$CH_4 + 2O_2 = CO_2 + 2H_2O$

When bonds change, electrons move between orbits in the outer layers of the atoms. This can happen only when the molecules or atoms come very close to each other, such as when they collide.

Reaction rates

Molecules collide more often when they are more concentrated; that is, when there are more of them in a given volume. So at higher concentrations, the reactants have more chance of colliding and then reacting together. If a reaction involves two reactants and the concentration of one reactant is doubled, the reaction rate will be twice as fast. But if the concentrations of both reactants are doubled, the rate will be four times as fast. Similarly, increasing the density of gaseous reactants by compressing them usually helps a reaction go faster. At room temperature of 77°F (25°C) and normal air pressure, an oxygen molecule will travel on average 3 millionths of an inch (7.3 millionths of a centimeter) before colliding, and will have some 6.6 billion collisions per second. If the pressure is doubled, it will travel half as far between collisions on average, and will collide twice as often.

If the gas is at a higher temperature, its molecules move faster. Greater molecular speeds make a reaction go faster for two reasons. First, the faster molecules travel, the more frequently they will collide. However,

> ### SCIENCE WORDS
>
> - **Activated complex:** A short-lived molecule formed during a reaction that quickly breaks up into either the original reactant molecules or into product molecules.
> - **Activation energy:** The difference between the average energy of reactant molecules at a given temperature and the energy they need to react.
> - **Catalyst:** A substance that speeds up a chemical reaction, but is not used up in the process.

CHEMICAL REACTIONS

Some chemical reactions—like this explosion—take place very fast, with dramatic effects. Others happen so slowly that chemists try to find ways to speed them up.

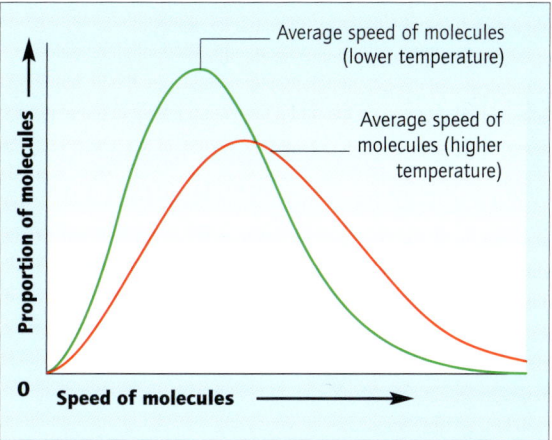

As the temperature increases, the average speed of molecules increases, as does the proportion with higher speeds. The range of speeds also rises with temperature, so the graph is more spread out at the higher temperature (red line) than at the lower temperature (green line).

this makes only a very small contribution to reaction rates. If the temperature of a gas (at atmospheric pressure) is raised from 77°F (25°C) to 95°F (35°C), there will be only about 2 percent more collisions per second.

Second and more important is the fact that, when molecules collide at higher speeds, they are more likely to interact. The molecules will have more energy to break and make bonds, rather than just bouncing off each other. However, at all temperatures there is a spread of molecular speeds, from very slow to very fast. There are always a few molecules traveling quick enough to react if they collide, even at lower temperatures.

Another factor influencing reaction rates is how easy it is for the reactants to mix. If all the reactants are liquids or gases, they will mix easily. But if one is a solid, it may need to be ground up into small pieces to increase the area of its surface exposed to the other reactants. A large lump of a solid substance will react more slowly than the same substance in powdered form. For this reason, chemists often use powdered chemicals, rather than lumps or large crystals.

Finally, adding a catalyst can speed up a reaction. Catalysts are substances that change the rate of a chemical reaction, but are not used up in the process.

INCREASING REACTION RATES

There are four main ways to increase the rate of a reaction: the substances can be heated (1); mixed in a more finely divided form (2); or a catalyst can be added (3); or used at higher concentrations (4).

RATES OF REACTIONS

Reaction curves

To measure how fast a reaction is taking place, we need to measure either how fast one or more of the products is being formed, or the rate at which a reactant is being used up. This means finding out how much of a product is present, or how much of a reactant is left, at different times. That is done by taking measurements at set intervals of time. For example, the compound hydrogen peroxide, H_2O_2, breaks down to form oxygen and water. (This reaction happens very slowly at room temperature, but it can be speeded up by raising the temperature or adding a catalyst.) If we plot a graph of the measured concentrations of hydrogen peroxide against the time elapsed, this will make a curve that shows the rates of reaction as the breakdown process occurs.

On Graph 1 below, the concentration of hydrogen peroxide is highest at the start of the reaction. It gradually falls over time as the hydrogen peroxide breaks

This graph shows how the concentration of products increases during the course of a reaction. The rate at which the reaction proceeds falls as the reactants are used up.

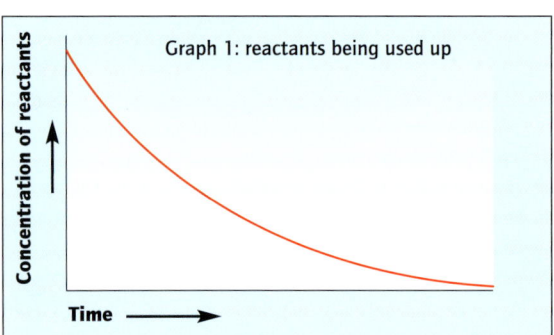

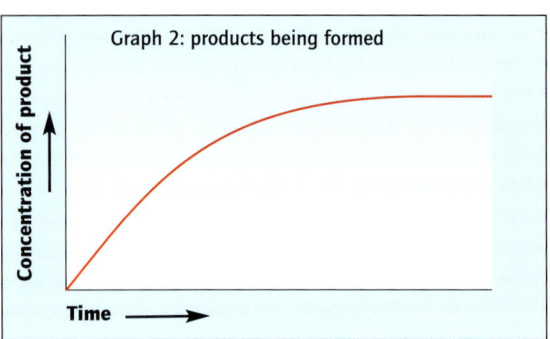

TRY THIS

Rate of rusting

In the rusting activity on page 10, we saw how iron and oxygen reacted to make iron oxide, or rust. You can repeat this reaction to investigate how different conditions affect the rate of reaction. You'll need three jars and three new nails. In jar 1, repeat the activity as before. Ask an adult to cover the nail in jar 2 with boiled water and put the lid on. In jar 3, place a nail with no water and put the lid on. Return after a day and compare the results.

By changing the conditions, you change the rate of the reaction. The nail in jar 1 will have rusted as before. The boiled water in jar 2 contains very little oxygen, so hardly any rust will form. The reaction runs faster in wet conditions, so very little rust will have formed in jar 3. But over a long time, moisture in the air may help the nail rust.

down. The slope of the curve is steepest at the start of the reaction, showing that the breakdown reaction is fastest when hydrogen peroxide levels are highest.

If we look at products being formed in a reaction, rather than reactants disappearing, the reaction curve will be a different shape. For example, imagine that two reactants react together to form two products. If we plotted a diagram of the concentration of one product against time, it might look like Graph 2 (left).

There, the reaction is also fastest at the start, where the curve is steepest. On this curve the concentration is rising, because the curve shows the product being formed during the reaction rather than the reactant disappearing. As the reaction carries on, the reactants are used up and the rate slows down, so the curve levels off. Eventually no more products are formed, so the reaction curve becomes a straight, flat line.

Activation energy

When two molecules collide, they sometimes stick together to form a temporary molecule. These temporary, intermediate molecules, called activated complexes, often have high energy and cannot exist for long. Instead, they break down into product molecules or turn back into the reactant molecules.

This process is very important in reactions. Imagine that two molecules collide to form an activated complex. After a short time this breaks down to form the product molecules. To form the activated complex, the reactants need to take in a certain amount of energy. The difference between this energy and the average energy of the reactant molecules is called the activation energy. The larger this is, the more slowly the activated complex will be formed.

In this case, the reaction will not happen spontaneously, even if it is exothermic (that is, the products have less energy than the reactants). The molecules need to be supplied with the activation energy before the reaction can start. This is like an oil drum lying in a hollow at the top of a hill: it needs to be pushed out of the hollow before it can roll downhill. The energy that it is given to lift it to the top of the bump is like the activation energy needed to form the activated complex.

If a reaction as a whole is exothermic, energy is given out between the initial and the final stages. So, when the activated complex breaks down in an exothermic reaction, it releases more energy than it absorbed when it was formed. This is why the reaction as a whole gives out energy. But if the chemical reaction is endothermic (absorbing energy), the activated complex releases less energy when it breaks down than was used in forming it. Many catalysts work by lowering the activation energy of a reaction, so the reaction can start more easily and the products form faster.

Equilibrium

If the conditions are right, many reactions go to completion. That is, they continue until the reactants are almost completely used up. However, other reactions do not continue so far. They reach a point where no more products seem to be formed, even though there are still reactants present.

EQUILIBRIUM IN EVAPORATION AND FREEZING

Equilibrium occurs in physical processes as well as chemical reactions. If a liquid is stored in a closed container, it begins to evaporate. The number of vapor molecules above the liquid increases and they reenter the liquid more and more frequently. Equilibrium is reached when as many molecules leave the liquid each second as enter it from the vapor. The vapor is then described as saturated.

Under ordinary conditions, liquid water cannot exist below 32°F (0°C). Similarly, ice (solid water) cannot exist above this temperature. So ice floating in water is at equilibrium: the temperature cannot go higher until all the ice has melted, and it cannot go lower until all the water has frozen. If a small amount of heat flows into or out of the system, the ice will melt or the water will freeze, but the temperature will not change.

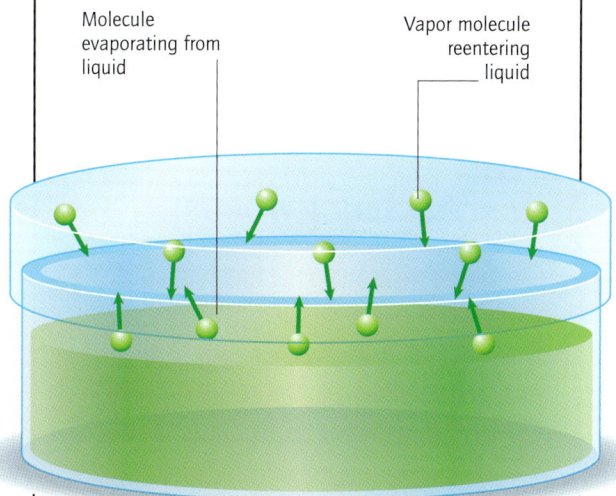

At equilibrium, as many molecules are moving back into the liquid as are moving out of the liquid into the vapor.

RATES OF REACTIONS

In fact, what is happening is that the products are still being formed—but these are reacting together to produce the reactants again, at the same rate. When reactants and products are being formed at exactly the same rate, the amount of each stays the same. This is what chemists call a reaction in equilibrium (balance).

An extremely important industrial reaction that reaches equilibrium is that of nitrogen gas (N_2) with hydrogen gas (H_2) to form ammonia (NH_3):

$$N_2 + 3H_2 \rightarrow 2NH_3$$

This is called the forward reaction. At the beginning only hydrogen and nitrogen are present, but soon ammonia molecules are formed. As the ammonia molecules build up, they collide with each other more frequently and some of them break down into nitrogen and hydrogen:

$$2NH_3 \rightarrow N_2 + 3H_2$$

This is called the reverse reaction. It will go faster as the amount of ammonia increases, and eventually ammonia molecules will be breaking down as fast as new ones are made. At equilibrium there will be a mixture of nitrogen, hydrogen, and ammonia molecules.

To show that the reactions in both directions are occurring at the same time, chemists write this reaction using a double-headed arrow:

$$N_2 + 3H_2 \rightarrow 2NH_3$$

> ### SCIENCE WORDS
> - **Reaction rate:** The rate at which the concentrations of reactants and products change during the reaction.
> - **Reversible reaction:** A reaction that can go both forward and backward. In other words, as well as the reactants forming the products (as in all reactions), the products react together to re-form the reactants in significant amounts.

Moving the equilibrium point

If the temperature or pressure of a two-way reaction changes, the equilibrium amounts of the initial reactants and the final products will also change. Exactly how the equilibrium point is affected is complex, and it depends on the details of the particular reaction concerned. For example, in the production of ammonia, increasing the temperature causes less ammonia to form. By contrast, when carbon burns to form carbon monoxide, the equilibrium shifts toward increased production of carbon monoxide when the temperature increases.

Adding a catalyst will not alter the position of any equilibrium—that is, the amount of reactants and products. Catalysts speed up the rate of a reversible reaction in both directions. That is why they do not change the concentrations at equilibrium—although equilibrium can be reached sooner with a catalyst.

In any reaction, if the amount of products at equilibrium increases, chemists say that the equilibrium has shifted to the right (because the products are on the right of the equation). If a change in conditions makes more reactants form, they say that the equilibrium has moved to the left.

Le Châtelier's principle

The French chemist Henri Louis Le Châtelier (1850–1936) formulated a rule that is very helpful in understanding how a chemical equilibrium will be affected by any changes. This rule states that, when a chemical system in equilibrium is disturbed, it changes in a way that tends to cancel out the disturbance.

For example, increasing the pressure makes gases dissolve or combine with other substances. So, the number of gas molecules is reduced. This tends to reduce the pressure, reducing the effect of the change in pressure. Similarly, increasing the temperature makes endothermic (heat-absorbing) reactions go faster, which has the effect of reducing the temperature.

In the formation of ammonia from nitrogen and hydrogen, heat is produced (because the forward

CHEMICAL REACTIONS

THE HABER–BOSCH PROCESS

Gaseous ammonia (NH_3) is a valuable industrial product. It is used in fertilizers, explosives, cleaning products, making batteries, and many other processes and products. Ammonia is made on a huge scale from nitrogen obtained from the air, plus hydrogen (mostly produced from naturally occurring methane). Before ammonia was produced by the Haber–Bosch process, the main industrial sources of nitrogen compounds were minerals that had to be mined and transported thousands of miles. By 1913, the research of two German chemists had made the industrial production of ammonia possible. Fritz Haber (1868–1934) studied the reaction in the laboratory, and Carl Bosch (1874–1940) of the company BASF turned it into an industrial process. Haber worked on the reversible reaction:

$$N_2 + 3H_2 \rightarrow 2NH_3$$

The problem was that, as more ammonia was produced, it increasingly turned back into nitrogen and hydrogen. Bosch made this reaction go to completion by removing the ammonia as it was produced, through cooling and liquefying it. The unreacted nitrogen and hydrogen were recycled, so that eventually they were all used up.

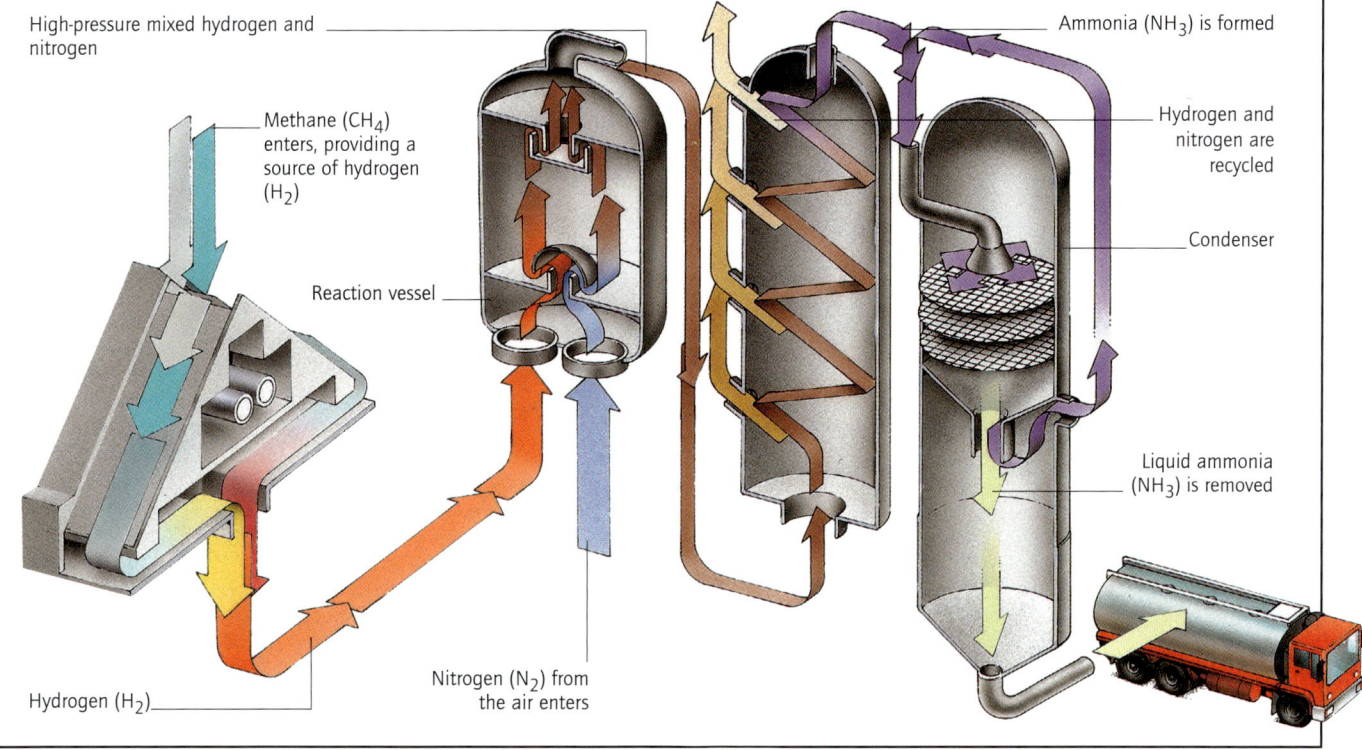

reaction is exothermic), and the volume decreases (because two molecules of ammonia are produced from four molecules of nitrogen and hydrogen). Here, Le Châtelier's principle tells us that raising the pressure will shift the equilibrium toward the production of ammonia. This is because ammonia takes up less volume than the reactants (nitrogen and hydrogen), so forming ammonia reduces the pressure. But raising the temperature will shift the equilibrium in the opposite direction—toward more nitrogen and hydrogen and less ammonia—so that less heat is given out and the temperature is lowered.

CATALYSTS

Chemists need to be able to control which reactions happen and how fast they go. Catalysts provide a very important way of controlling reactions.

Our lives depend on how fast chemical reactions proceed. Within our own bodies, countless different chemical reactions are going on at every moment. Most of these would happen far too slowly by themselves. In industry, many reactions are speeded up so that they produce a worthwhile amount of product within a reasonable time. Industrial chemists find ways to make reactions happen fast and safely.

A very useful way to speed up chemical reactions is to add a catalyst. Although a catalyst can help a reaction proceed faster, at the end of the reaction none of the catalyst will have been used up.

Catalysts in action

People have been using catalysts in traditional foodmaking for thousands of years. In making beer, wine, and other alcoholic drinks, natural sugars such as glucose are broken down into carbon dioxide and ethanol (alcohol). The sugars are broken down by single-celled fungi called yeasts, which produce natural catalysts that promote these reactions. Yeast is also used in baking bread; the bubbles of carbon dioxide that yeast releases within the dough cause the bread to rise (swell up). Catalysts are just as important in the modern industrial processes used to produce much of the food we eat today.

In the petrochemical industry, a vast range of products are made from petroleum (oil extracted from the ground) using catalysts. The products include gasoline, lubrication oil, gas for heating and lighting, and plastics. All these materials and products are made from gases and liquids produced from petroleum. This mixture of compounds has molecules of different size. First, petroleum is heated so that the compounds with the smallest molecules can be driven off as gases; these are collected and separated from the remaining mixture. Then, the larger molecules in the mixture are chemically broken to form smaller, more useful molecules; this process is called cracking. Some other molecules may need to be joined together, or reshaped, to get the best blend of compounds. In these molecule-forming processes, chemical engineers use carefully chosen catalysts to control the types and amounts of products.

Catalysts are just as important in many other industrial processes. In the Haber–Bosch process for making ammonia (see page 47), finely divided iron mixed with oxides of potassium, calcium, and aluminum is used as the catalyst. Vanadium oxide

CHEMICAL REACTIONS

(V_2O_5) is the catalyst used in the contact process for making sulfuric acid. Margarine is made by adding hydrogen to oils and fats; the metal nickel is used as a catalyst for this reaction.

How catalysts work

Some catalysts are gases or liquids that are mixed uniformly with reactants that are also gases or liquids. These are called homogeneous catalysts. They enable intermediate molecules called activated complexes to form with a lower energy than the intermediate molecules in the unaided reaction. Because they have a lower energy, these intermediate complexes form more rapidly, and so do the final products.

At this brewery in the Netherlands, the beer's alcoholic content is produced by yeasts, which ferment the natural sugars in the mix.

Other catalysts are heterogeneous, which means that the catalyst is in one physical form—usually solid—and the reactants are in another (such as gases or liquids). The precious metals platinum and rhodium are used as heterogeneous catalysts in devices called catalytic converters. These devices are used in automobiles to help the fuel burn completely and to break down poisonous gases in the exhaust fumes.

For example, nitric oxide (NO) is one of the gases that can cause pollution from car exhaust fumes. When nitric oxide molecules meet the metal in a catalytic converter, they are "adsorbed" onto it; that is, they are attached to its surface. On the metal surface, the nitric oxide molecules break down into individual atoms of nitrogen and oxygen. This may take place at only a small number of places, called active sites, on the surface of the catalytic converter. The nitrogen and oxygen atoms, being close to each other, can then combine to form nitrogen (N_2) and oxygen (O_2) molecules:

Petroleum is processed industrially in huge refineries. The process includes "cracking," in which large molecules are broken down, using catalysts, to form smaller ones.

49

CATALYSTS

CATALYTIC CONVERTER

1 Nitric oxide (NO) molecule — Catalyst

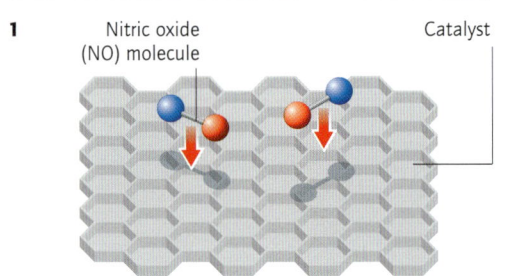

(1) In a catalytic converter, nitric oxide (NO) molecules arrive at the catalyst and attach to its surface.

2 Nitrogen atom — Oxygen atom

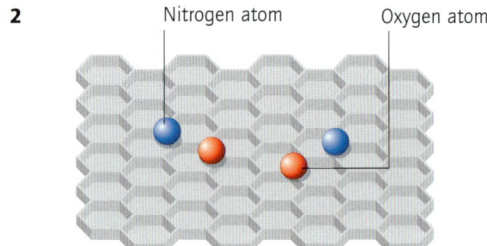

(2) The nitric oxide molecules separate into atoms of nitrogen and oxygen.

3 Oxygen molecule — Nitrogen molecule

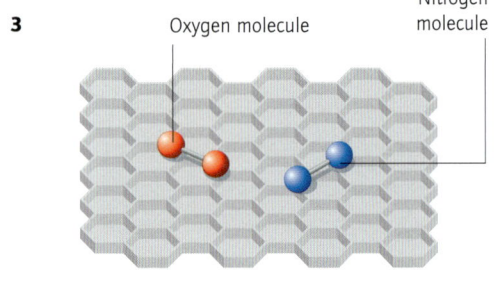

(3) Molecules of nitrogen (N_2) and oxygen (O_2) gas are formed.

4

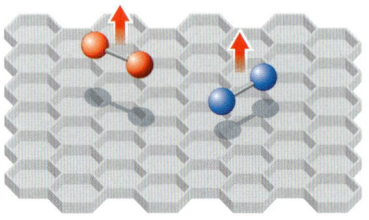

(4) The new gas molecules detach and move away.

$$2NO \rightarrow N_2 + O_2$$

Another process that takes place in catalytic converters combines oxygen and poisonous carbon monoxide (CO) into carbon dioxide (CO_2), which is safe:

$$2CO + O_2 \rightarrow 2CO_2$$

The catalytic converter also helps any traces of fuel present in the exhaust gases burn completely. For example, octane (C_8H_{18}) can be burned to form carbon dioxide and water:

$$2C_8H_{18} + 25O_2 \rightarrow 16CO_2 + 18H_2O$$

Notice that this involves the reaction of two octane molecules with no fewer than 25 oxygen molecules. On the surface of the catalytic converter, the reaction goes through a long series of steps. At each step, oxygen molecules come into contact with partially burned fuel molecules formed in the previous step, allowing further burning to take place. This means that the fuel is burned more completely, reducing pollution.

An illustration of the inside of a car's catalytic converter. The engine exhaust passes through a mesh coated in platinum and iridium. These catalysts turn the pollution in the exhaust, such as nitrogen oxides (NO_x), unburned hydrocarbons (HC), and carbon monoxide (CO), into less harmful gases, such as carbon dioxide (CO_2), water (H_2O), and nitrogen (N_2).

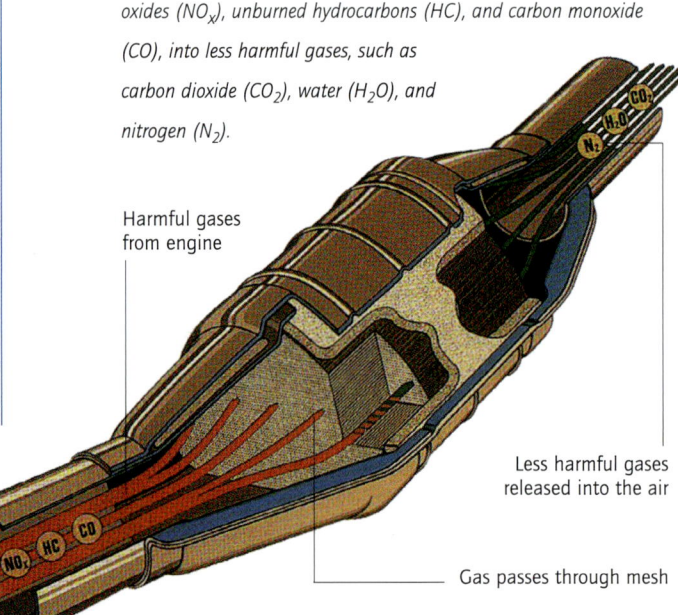

Harmful gases from engine

Less harmful gases released into the air

Gas passes through mesh

CHEMICAL REACTIONS

Computer-generated model of the bacterial enzyme purine nucleoside phosphorylase, which is used in the design of anti-cancer and immunosuppressant drugs.

Enzymes

The most extraordinary examples of catalysts are those called enzymes, which are found in living things. Enzymes are protein molecules, and like other proteins they are made up of long, folded chains of repeated chemical units called amino acids.

Enzymes make it possible for the body to break down food molecules, destroy toxic molecules, rebuild molecules needed elsewhere in the body, and do many other things. Their actions are incredibly precise: each enzyme targets particular molecules so only a specific reaction is affected.

For example, amylase is a digestive enzyme present in human saliva. It breaks down starch to form maltose (a sugar consisting of two glucose molecules joined together). Similarly, the enzyme catalase, found in the blood, catalyzes the breakdown of harmful hydrogen peroxide (H_2O_2), which can build up in the body as a result of natural processes, to form oxygen and water. Hydrogen peroxide is also sometimes used on skin wounds as a disinfectant: the enzyme's action makes it bubble vigorously.

Sugars, enzymes, and milk

Our bodies need to obtain the sugar glucose from our food. Food often contains complex sugars, in which the molecules consist of simple sugars (such as glucose) joined together. For example, human and cow's milk contains lactose, in which glucose is combined with another simple sugar, galactose. The enzyme lactase in the human body breaks down lactose into glucose and galactose molecules.

Some people do not make enough lactase to break down lactose. If they drink milk, they feel ill. They can drink soy milk instead, which is made from the soy plant. In fact, lactose intolerance is surprisingly "normal": the people of many ethnic groups in the world can only digest milk in childhood and lose this ability when they become adults.

SCIENCE WORDS

- **Active site:** The place on an enzyme or other catalyst where the reactants attach and the reaction occurs.
- **Adsorption:** The process of molecules becoming attached to a surface.
- **Enzyme:** A biological protein that acts as a catalyst.
- **Inhibitor:** A substance that slows down a chemical reaction without being used up by it; also called a negative catalyst.
- **Protein:** A substance consisting of large molecules made up of chains of chemical units called amino acids.
- **Substrate:** The particular molecule on which an enzyme acts.

CATALYSTS

How enzymes work

Enzymes work by a so-called "lock-and-key" mechanism. Each enzyme molecule has a particular place on it that acts as the "lock." Certain reactant molecules are like keys: these molecules—and no others—fit into the "lock" region of the enzyme, which is the active site. The "key" molecules are known as substrates.

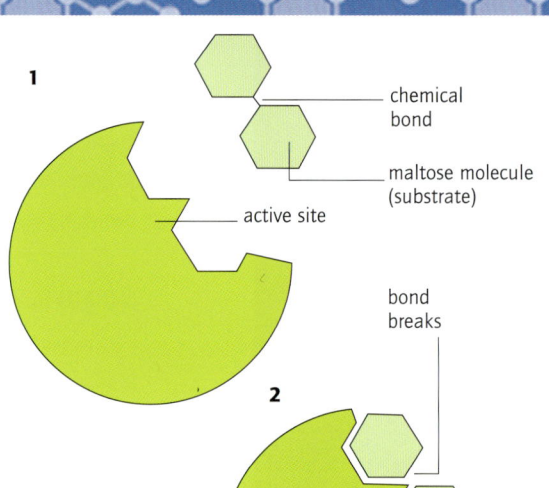
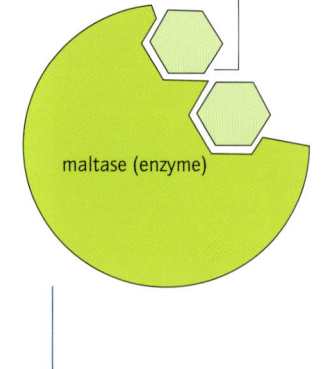
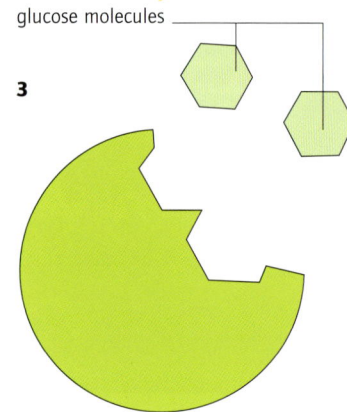

The enzyme maltase breaks down maltose to form glucose. A maltose molecule approaches the enzyme (1) and attaches to the active site (2). After reaction, the glucose molecules are released (3).

When an enzyme catalyzes a chemical reaction, the enzyme molecule is in contact with all kinds of reactant molecules. Only the substrate molecules that encounter the active site are adsorbed (stick) there. In a breakdown reaction, the enzyme structure helps the bonds in the adsorbed substrate molecules break. The molecules can then split apart, and finally the parts separate from the enzyme molecule.

In a reaction where two substrates combine, a molecule of one of the substrates will be first to reach the enzyme's active site and stick there. Later, a molecule of the second substrate will encounter the enzyme at the right place and be adsorbed. Having been brought together, the two substrate molecules react with each other, forming the product molecule. That then separates from the enzyme.

Enzymes in technology

Enzymes are essential to every living organism, and scientists and engineers are increasingly finding uses for enzymes in industry and advanced technology. For example, enzymes are now used in making laundry

NOT TOO HOT AND NOT TOO COLD

The catalytic activity of an enzyme is reduced or destroyed if the temperature is too cold or too hot. Warm-blooded animals, such as humans, are those that can control their internal temperatures to keep them in the right range for enzyme activity. "Cold-blooded" animals, such as reptiles, are not really cold-blooded: they too have to keep the enzymes in their system working by keeping the inside of their body reasonably warm. They do this by generating heat through muscular activity, or by moving into sunshine or shade as needed.

An iguana basking in the sunshine on a warm rock; this helps keep its body temperature right for enzyme activity.

CHEMICAL REACTIONS

TRY THIS

Testing for glucose in milk

First, pour half a cup of water into a beaker or glass. Add a tablespoon of glucose and stir well, then dip a glucose test strip (from drugstores) into the solution. Compare its color with the key on the package to find out the amount of glucose in the solution (and write down the result).

Next, put some soy milk into a cup, test with a fresh test strip and write down the result. Then put some cow's milk into a cup and test that with another strip, noting the result. Finally, add a few lactase drops (an enzyme available from drugstores) to the ordinary milk, stir it up, test it again with another strip, and note the result.

Looking at your results, which liquid had the most glucose and which the least? How did the glucose level change when you added the lactase drops to the milk?

You should have found that there was almost no glucose in the ordinary milk (and much less than in the glucose and water mixture). This is because ordinary milk contains little glucose; its sugar is in the form of lactose. Adding lactase breaks down lactose into glucose and galactose, so there should be more glucose in the milk and lactase mixture than in the ordinary milk. There should be no glucose in the soy milk, which contains only other sweeteners.

Comparing the colors on the test strips with those on the key reveals the concentration of glucose in each of the beakers.

powders, food, cosmetics, and medicines. One advantage of using enzymes to catalyze industrial reactions is that they can make reactions happen under mild conditions, rather than at the high temperatures and pressures often used in industry. Another advantage is that enzymes can be much cheaper than the hugely expensive precious metals that are often used as catalysts.

An exciting possibility is that enzymes may become a vital part of nanotechnology, in which machines are built on the molecular scale. Already "DNA computers," which use enzymes and can make calculations in a test tube, have been built. Some researchers think that, in the future, tiny enzyme-and-DNA computers could be embedded in our body to monitor health and release drugs to repair damaged or unhealthy tissue.

ELECTROCHEMISTRY

Chemical reactions can generate electricity. Reacting electrons are forced to flow in one direction, creating an electric current. The current is then used to power machines.

Electrochemistry uses redox reactions to produce electricity. Remember that a redox reaction happens when electrons move from one compound to another. In electrochemistry, the electrons that are exchanged during redox reactions are forced to travel from one place to another. These traveling, charged particles create an electric current.

Redox is short for reduction-oxidation, the two halves of the reaction. The reduction occurs when one compound gains electrons. The oxidation occurs when one compound loses electrons. Chemists use something called a voltaic cell to harness the electricity produced

Dry batteries like those shown here contain chemicals that produce electric currents when they react.

by the reactions. Voltaic cells are named for Alessandro Volta (1745–1827), an Italian count who invented them in 1799. The volt (V), the unit used for measuring the strength of an electric current, is also named for him.

Voltaic cell

A voltaic cell is a pump that forces electrons to move from one place to another. In a simple cell, there are two dishes of chemical solutions connected by a U-shaped pipeline. One dish is where the reduction reaction takes place; the other dish is where the oxidation reaction takes place. The electrons must travel between the two dishes through the pipeline. The pipeline is filled with a solution of ions to carry the electrons.

Each dish contains a stick of metal called an electrode. Metals are good conductors of electricity because they have many free-floating electrons inside.

DRY BATTERY

A dry battery as used in a flashlight is a type of Leclanché cell that has a paste of ammonium chloride as the electrolyte.

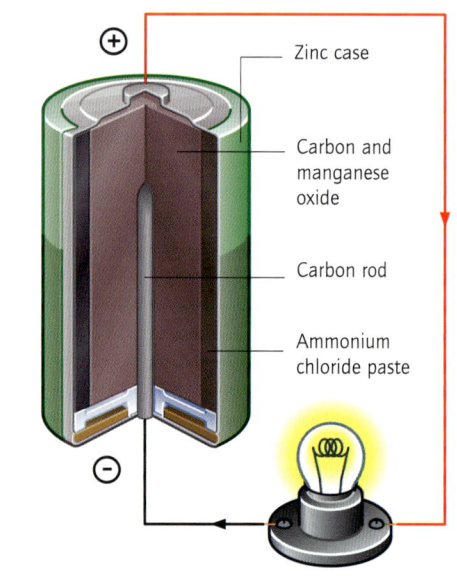

CHEMICAL REACTIONS

TRY THIS

Fruit power

You can make a voltaic cell with a citrus fruit. Press a lemon on the table and roll it to release the juice. Push a 2-inch- (5-cm-) long copper wire into the side of the lemon. This is your cathode. Push a straightened paper clip into the lemon next to the copper wire. This is your anode. They should both be 1 inch (2.5 cm) deep and must not touch.

Touch your tongue to the cathode and anode at the same time. What do you feel? A reaction in the cell releases electrons that move through your tongue. You should feel a slight tingling, but it will not hurt.

The metal electrodes serve as a holding tank of electrons, ready to carry a current when needed once they are connected to each other with a wire.

The electrode where the reduction reaction takes place is called the cathode. The cathode is usually labeled with a "−" because the current of electrons flows away from it. The oxidation-reaction electrode is called the anode. The anode is labeled with a "+" because the current flows toward it.

The electrodes are immersed in a liquid that contains the reactants for the redox reaction. The two halves of the reaction happen continuously until one of the reactants runs out. In the reduction reaction, a reactant gains electrons from the anode to become the product. This product then joins onto the anode, gradually building up a thin layer. In this way the anode is constantly supplying the reactants with electrons. At the cathode, the opposite happens. The reactant is being oxidized and is giving away electrons. The cathode collects these electrons.

The electrons flow through the wire between the electrodes. Electrons are negatively charged, so they flow away from the negative cathode to the positive anode. The current contains energy and this energy can be transported along wires to provide power to run machines.

Voltaic cells can use many different types of chemicals in the redox reactions, but they often contain metals. One reaction involves zinc and manganese dioxide. The pure zinc is oxidized into zinc hydroxide and releases electrons. The manganese dioxide is reduced into manganese trioxide and gains electrons.

Modern batteries

A battery is a portable voltaic cell. Batteries come in many shapes, sizes, and powers, but they all work by storing chemical energy and turning it into electrical energy using a redox reaction.

All batteries contain an anode (the flat, negative end) and a cathode (the raised, positive end). Instead of a U-shaped tube, the electrodes are separated by a mixture of chemicals called electrolytes. Electrolytes contain ions. Ions are formed when atoms gain or lose electrons. This gives the atoms a charge. Positive ions have lost electrons, while negative ions have gained

55

ELECTROCHEMISTRY

them. The ions flow through the electrolyte and carry the charge between the electrodes.

When a battery is sitting on a table, the redox reaction is not happening inside because there is nothing connecting the anode and cathode. When you put your battery into a device, such as a flashlight, you create a path between the anode and cathode. That completes a circuit and the redox reaction begins. The circuit is a circular path through which electricity can flow. If there is a break in the circuit the electricity will not flow.

When the redox reaction begins inside the battery, electricity is produced. A fixed amount of reactants is stored in the battery. When the reactants are completely used up, we say the battery is "dead." A dead battery can no longer produce electricity because the chemical reaction is not taking place.

Some batteries are rechargeable. They work in the same way as a regular battery. However, when a rechargeable battery becomes dead, you plug it into an electrical outlet. Electricity from the outlet forces all the reactions inside a rechargeable battery to run in reverse. The anode becomes the cathode, the cathode becomes the anode, and the products of the reaction become the reactants. This generates a new source of the original reactants so the battery can make electricity again.

SCIENCE WORDS

- **Anode:** Where oxidation reactions occur in a voltaic cell.
- **Cathode:** Where reduction reactions occur in a voltaic cell.
- **Electrode:** A storage tank for electrons in a voltaic cell.
- **Electrolyte liquid:** Containing ions that carry a current between electrodes.
- **Voltage:** The force that pushes electrons through an electric circuit.

Michael Faraday

English chemist and physicist Michael Faraday (1791–1867) is remembered for investigating electromagnetism and electrochemistry. The son of a blacksmith, Faraday taught himself about chemistry by reading books and by helping out in laboratories as a boy. As an adult, he established the laws of electrolysis and established the link between electricity and magnetism. He made the first electric motor and generator and coined the terms *electrolyte*, *electrode*, *anode*, and *cathode*.

Electrolytic cells

Electrolytic cells are the opposite of voltaic cells. Voltaic cells use a redox reaction to produce electricity. Electrolytic cells use electricity to produce a redox reaction. Electrolysis is a process of pushing electricity through a solution to force a reaction to occur. The reaction generally involves a stable compound being broken apart. The word electrolysis means "splitting with electricity." During the electrolysis of water, for example, water molecules are broken into their hydrogen and oxygen atoms. Chemists run electricity through liquid water to start the reaction, which has the basic equation:

$2H_2O \rightarrow 2H_2 + O_2$

Like all redox reactions, the electrolysis of water has two halves. The water is reduced at the cathode. The molecules receive electrons. This causes them to split into hydrogen gas (H_2) and hydroxide ions (OH^-):

$2H_2O + 2 \text{ electrons} \rightarrow H_2 + 2OH^-$

The ions stay in the the water, but the hydrogen forms gas bubbles on the electrode.

At the anode the water is oxidized: electrons are released by the water molecules to make oxygen atoms and hydrogen ions (H^+):

$2H_2O \rightarrow O_2 + 4H^+ + 4 \text{ electrons}$

CHEMICAL REACTIONS

The oxygen bubbles out of the liquid like the hydrogen. The electrons travel along a wire to the cathode and take part in the reduction of more water molecules.

Fuel cell

A hydrogen fuel cell uses hydrogen and oxygen gas to make electricity. A hydrogen fuel cell is like a battery, but has a different source of reactants. A battery has reactants stored inside. Space is limited, and when the reactants run out, the battery becomes dead. The reactants for a fuel cell are stored outside and pumped into the cell, so space is not a problem. In a hydrogen fuel cell, hydrogen and oxygen are combined to form water. As they react, the energy released is used to produce electricity. Fuel cells are an attractive source of power because they do not produce any harmful pollution, just water vapor.

Electrochemistry and metals

Electrolysis is used to separate pure metals (elements) from their compounds. That is called electrorefining. The process used is the same as the one used to break water apart. In nature, most metals are found as compounds. Electrolysis is often the only way to extract reactive metals.

The metal compounds are dissolved or melted to make an electrolyte. Electrolysis provides the energy needed to remove the metal atoms from the compound. The metal atoms collect at one electrode. Waste material forms at the other.

The same electrolysis process is used to cover objects with a thin layer of metal. This is called electroplating. When you buy an inexpensive gold necklace, it is likely to be another type of metal covered with a very thin layer of gold.

During the electroplating process, the object to be coated becomes the cathode. The valuable metal used for coating is the anode and this is also dissolved in the electrolyte. Electrolysis deposits the anode metal onto the cathode.

TRY THIS

Pile of coins

Electric batteries were once called piles because they were made from stacks, or piles, of voltaic cells. You can make your own pile using a stack of pennies and dimes, paper towel, and some concentrated lemon juice. The coins are the electrodes; the penny is the anode and the dime the cathode. The lemon juice is the electrolyte.

Cut the paper towel into about ten 1-inch (2.5-cm) squares. Soak these pieces in the lemon juice so they are sopping wet. Use a strong paper towel so it does not break apart when wet. Clip one end of an electric wire to a penny, and begin building a stack in this order: penny, dime, paper towel, penny, dime, paper towel, and so on. Use all the paper towel pieces and end with a dime on top. Connect a second wire to this top dime.

Connect the loose ends of the wires to an ammeter. Switch the wires if you do not get a reading. You can repeat the experiment using salty water instead of lemon juice. The piles could also be made with aluminum foil and iron nails. These changes will result in a slightly different size of electric current.

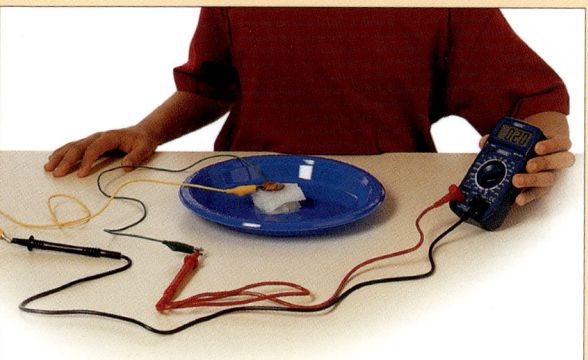

An electric battery made from pennies and dimes. A pair of coins on top of each other makes a single cell. The paper towel is used to divide one cell from another. The juice can pass through the paper, and so an electric current will run through the whole pile. Connect an inexpensive ammeter or voltmeter to see how much current is produced.

NUCLEAR REACTIONS

Nuclear reactions turn one element into another element, releasing enormous amounts of energy in the process. Chemists study how to control nuclear reactions safely so that they can be used to create energy.

Nuclear reactions are reactions that involve the particles inside the nucleus of an atom. All chemical reactions only involve the electrons in the space surrounding the nucleus. None affect the nucleus itself. Nuclear reactions are different because they change one element into another by changing the number of protons in the nucleus of the atom.

Unstable elements

Nuclear reactions involve a set of elements that chemists describe as radioactive. Radioactive elements have unstable atoms. The nuclei of these atoms often break apart, especially when they collide with another particle, such as a neutron. Elements with 83 or more protons in the nucleus are the most radioactive.

The instability is a result of there being so many protons packed into the nucleus. Protons are positively charged, so they are constantly pushing against each other. The reason they do not fly apart from each other is a stronger force that holds the protons and neutrons together. This force, called the strong nuclear force, only works over tiny distances. It has no effect outside the nucleus. In the nucleus of an unstable atom, the strong force is not powerful enough to keep all the particles together. Eventually the nucleus begins to break apart, or decay.

Radioactive decay occurs when the nucleus gives off small particles. These particles are also often called radiation. There are three types of radiation, each named after Greek letters: alpha, beta, and gamma. An alpha particle is two protons and two neutrons, a beta particle is a single electron, and a gamma ray is an emission of energy.

The Sun's heat and light are produced by nuclear reactions at its center.

Radiation

If you have already heard of nuclear reactions, it is probably because of the health concerns over radiation. High doses of radiation damage living cells so they die or cause dangerous illnesses.

Nuclear radiation burns the skin in the same way sunlight causes sunburn. Inside the body, radiation is more dangerous. It breaks up the contents of cells so they no longer work properly. The radiation may damage the cell's DNA, which causes the cell to work in the wrong way. DNA stands for deoxyribonucleic acid, which is the molecule that contains the information needed to organize a living cell. Damaged

CHEMICAL REACTIONS

NUCLEAR POWER

Nuclear power plants use the energy released by nuclear reactions to generate electricity. The heat from the reactions is used to boil water and make steam. The steam is used to spin large fans called a turbine. The turbine's spinning motion is converted into electricity by a generator. Coal and gas power plants do the same thing; they just use coal or oil fires to heat the water.

A diagram showing how the heat from nuclear reactions is used to make electricity.

Water tank

Nuclear reactions take place inside the reactor

Steam is piped to a turbine

Heat from reactor boils water

Turbine

Generator

DNA causes illnesses. For example the cell might begin to grow too quickly and become a cancerous tumor.

Radiation spills are a huge concern when building nuclear power plants. If something goes wrong in a such a power plant, radiation can be released into the air and harm living things in the area. For example, in 1986 an explosion at a reactor in Chernobyl, Ukraine, spread radiation over the homes of 200,000 people. All of them had to be evacuated.

Another major concern with nuclear power plants is the radioactive waste they produce. Nuclear reactions continue in this radioactive waste and can continue to emit dangerous amounts of radiation for 10,000 years or more. The waste must be stored for all that time. Despite the concerns over safety and the costs of storing waste, nuclear power produces less pollution than other methods.

Isotopes

Certain forms of the elements are more radioactive than others. The different forms of atoms are called isotopes. The number of protons in an atom determines what element it is. However, some atoms of the same element have different numbers of neutrons. This makes them different isotopes. Some isotopes are more radioactive than others because the number of neutrons makes them unstable.

To learn more about isotopes, it helps to understand how they are written. Chemists write isotopes in two ways. One way to write an isotope looks like this: $^a_z X$, where "X" is the chemical symbol, "z" is the atomic number—the number of protons in the nucleus, and "a" is the atomic mass number—the sum of the protons and neutrons in the nucleus. If you subtract the atomic number from the mass number, you get the number of neutrons in that isotope. This level of detail can be useful, but it is not always needed. Chemists may just write the symbol and the mass number, such as U-238 (uranium-238, or $^{238}_{92}U$).

When some isotopes start to decay, they sometimes cannot stop. For example, U-238 is an unstable isotope of uranium. When it begins to decay, it produces

NUCLEAR REACTIONS

thorium-234 (Th-234), another unstable isotope. Th-234 decays to protactinium-234 (Pa-234), yet another unstable isotope. The decay continues creating unstable isotopes until, after 14 unstable isotope steps, a stable atom is formed and the decay stops. Such a series of steps is known as a radioactive decay series, and is not unusual among the most unstable elements.

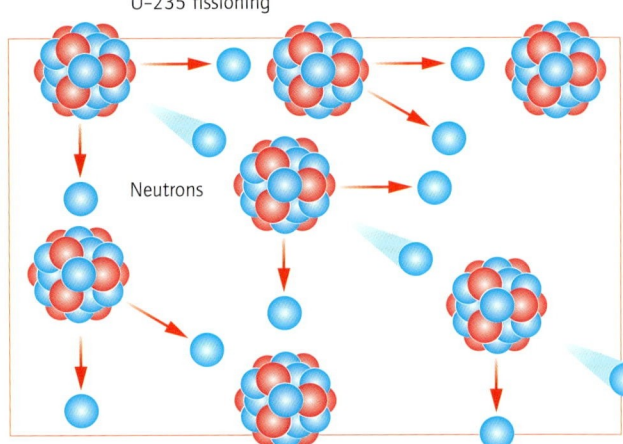

A diagram of how a nuclear fission can cause a chain reaction. A neutron hits a uranium-235 (U-235) nucleus. The nucleus splits in two and releases two or three neutrons. The neutrons then hit more U-235 atoms and cause yet more fission reactions.

Fission reactions

One type of nuclear reaction is called a fission reaction. A fission reaction occurs when a neutron strikes a large nucleus, breaking it into two or more new elements with smaller nuclei. In general, the equation for a fission reaction looks like this:

$$^a_z W + n \rightarrow {}^a_z X + {}^a_z Y + n$$

Element W is bombarded by a neutron (n), and produces two new elements, X and Y, plus more neutrons. As before, the numbers "a" and "z" represent the atomic mass and atomic number. (The atomic mass of a neutron is 1 and its atomic number is 0.)

> ### SCIENCE WORDS
> - **Atomic number:** The number of protons in the nucleus.
> - **Fission:** When a large atom breaks up into two small atoms.
> - **Fusion:** When small atoms fuse to make a single larger atom.
> - **Half-life:** The amount of time it takes for half the isotopes in a sample to break down.
> - **Isotope:** Atoms of the same element with different numbers of neutrons. Many isotopes are radioactive.
> - **Radioactive decay:** When small particles break off from an unstable nucleus.

Unlike a chemical reaction, which creates bonds between different elements, a fission reaction actually creates new elements. Fission reactions also release a lot of heat and several neutrons. These neutrons are then free to bombard other radioactive nuclei and start more fission reactions. That is a chain reaction. The nuclear reactors at power plants control the chain reaction so that the heat and radiation are released slowly and safely.

Fusion reactions

A fusion reaction is the opposite of a fission reaction. During fusion, two small nuclei combine to create a single large nucleus and release a lot of energy. Fusion reactions are very hard to start because they take huge amounts of energy to begin.

One place where fusion reactions happen continuously is inside the Sun. The Sun turns hydrogen

CHEMICAL REACTIONS

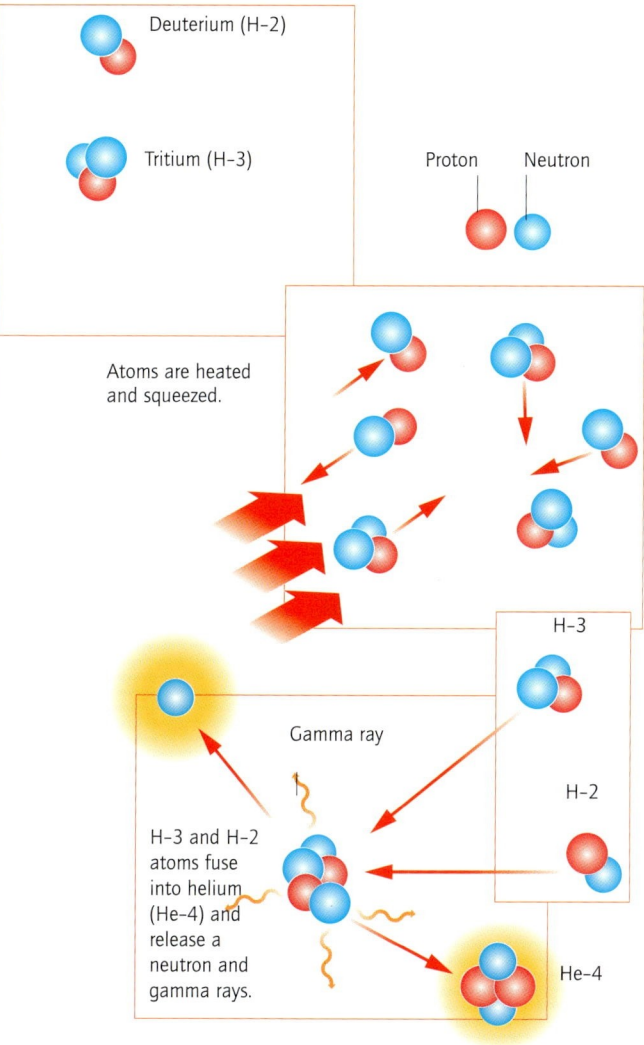

A diagram of the fusion reaction that takes place in the Sun. Two radioactive hydrogen isotopes—deuterium and tritium—fuse to make a single helium atom. Normal hydrogen atoms (H) have a single proton as a nucleus. Deuterium (H-2) has one proton and one neutron in the nucleus, while tritium (H-3) has one proton and two neutrons.

atoms into helium by fusion, and releases the energy that lights and warms our planet.

On Earth, scientists have experimented with ways to generate power from fusion reactions. Because the reactions require so much energy to get started, they are not easy to investigate. Fusion reactors are being built to test whether it is possible to release more energy from a fusion reaction than is added to start it. If this is achieved, fusion could be a useful new source of power.

Energy

You already know that the two fundamental components of the universe, matter and energy, interact during a chemical reaction. In a nuclear reaction, both matter and energy are still present and necessary, but the rules are different. Matter can be changed from one element to another during a nuclear reaction. But matter can also be changed into energy.

So much energy is released by a nuclear reaction because some of the matter in the original nucleus is converted into energy. Because chemists know the amount of mass involved, they can calculate the energy by using the famous equation, $E = mc^2$. E is energy, m is mass, and c is the speed of light. This equation was figured out by the great German-born American scientist Albert Einstein (1879-1955). The speed of light, it turns out, is a huge number and as a result small amounts of mass produce huge amounts of energy.

Balancing a nuclear equation

To balance a chemical equation you count atoms. To balance a nuclear equation you count the the number of subatomic particles.

The sum of all the atomic particles' numbers on the left-hand side must equal the sum of all particles on the right-hand side. None of the elements bond to make compounds, instead one element is changed into another element.

For example, when a uranium-235 (U-235) atom is hit by a neutron (n), a fission reaction occurs. U-235 breaks into two smaller elements, barium (Ba-142) and krypton (Kr-91):

$$^{235}_{92}U + n \rightarrow ^{142}_{56}Ba + ^{91}_{36}Kr + 3n$$

This equation is balanced. The number of particles in the reactants (235 + 1) is equal to the products (142 + 91 + 3).

GLOSSARY

Absolute zero The lowest theoretically possible temperature, −459.67°F (−273.15°C).

Activation energy The difference between the average energy of reactant molecules at a given temperature and the energy they need to react.

Active site The place on an enzyme or other catalyst where the reactants attach and the reaction occurs.

Adsorption The process of molecules becoming attached to a surface.

Anode Where oxidation reactions occur in a voltaic cell.

Atom The smallest piece of an element that still retains the properties of that element.

Atomic number The number of protons in the nucleus.

Bond A chemical link between atoms.

Calorimeter Apparatus for accurately measuring heat given out or taken in.

Catalyst A substance that speeds up a chemical reaction, but is not used up in the process.

Cathode Where reduction reactions occur in a voltaic cell.

Chemical equation Symbols and numbers that show how reactants change into products during a reaction.

Chemical formula A combination of chemical symbols that shows the type and number of elements in a molecule. H_2O is the formula for water, which contains two hydrogen (H) atoms and one oxygen (O).

Chemical symbol Letters used to represent a certain element, such as O for oxygen or Na for sodium.

Coefficient A number placed in front of a chemical formula to show how many molecules are used or produced by a reaction. $3H_2O$ stands for three water molecules.

Electrode A storage tank for electrons in a voltaic cell.

Electrolyte Liquid containing ions that carries a current between electrodes.

Electromagnetic radiation Radiation forming part of the electromagnetic spectrum, such as light and heat radiation.

Element A substance made up of just one type of atom.

Endothermic reaction One in which the reacting substances take in heat.

Energy The ability to cause a change in something by heating it up, altering its shape, or making it move.

Enthalpy change At constant pressure, the change in internal energy that occurs during any process.

Entropy A measure of the amount of disorder in any system.

Enzyme A biological protein that acts as a catalyst in biochemical reactions.

Exothermic reaction One in which the reacting substances give out heat.

Fission When a large atom breaks up into two small atoms.

Fusion When small atoms fuse to make a single larger atom.

Gibbs free energy A decrease in Gibbs free energy means that a reaction will happen spontaneously.

Half-life The amount of time it takes for half the isotopes in a sample to break down.

Heat capacity The amount of heat required to change the temperature of an object by 1°C (1.8°F).

Inhibitor A substance that slows down a chemical reaction without being used up by it; also called a negative catalyst.

Insoluble A substance that cannot dissolve.

Internal energy The total kinetic energy of all the particles in a system, plus all the chemical energy.

Isotope Atoms of the same element with different numbers of neutrons.

Kelvin scale Temperature scale that uses kelvins (K) as the unit of temperature, and where zero (0K) is absolute zero (−459.67°F; −273.15°C).

Kinetic energy The energy of movement.

Kinetic theory The study of heat flow and other processes in terms of the motion of the atoms and molecules involved.

Matter Anything that can be weighed.

Metal A hard but flexible element. Metals are good conductors. Their atoms have only a few outer electrons.

Metalloid An element that has both metallic and nonmetallic properties.

Microstate The state of a substance on the molecular scale—that is, the masses, speeds, and positions of all its molecules.

Molecule The smallest particle of a chemical substance that can exist on its own.

Nonmetal An element that is not a metal. Nonmetals are poor conductors. Their atoms tend to have several outer electrons.

Potential energy Energy that something has because of the way it is positioned or how its parts are arranged.

Precipitate An insoluble solid formed by a double displacement reaction between two dissolved compounds.

Products The substances produced in a chemical reaction.

Protein A substance consisting of large molecules made up of chains of chemical units called amino acids.

Radioactive decay When small particles break off from an unstable nucleus.

Reactants The substances that react together in a chemical reaction.

Reaction rate The rate at which the concentrations of reactants and products change during the reaction.

Reversible reaction A reaction that can go both forward and backward. In other words, as well as the reactants forming the products (as in all reactions), the products react together to re-form the reactants in significant amounts.

Solute The substance that dissolves in a solvent, to produce a solution.

Solution A mixture that contains a dissolved substance. Solids usually dissolve in liquids.

Solvent The liquid that solutes dissolve in.

Specific heat capacity The amount of heat required to change the temperature of a specified amount of a substance by 1°C (1.8°F).

Spontaneous reaction A reaction that happens by itself, without needing something from outside to start it off.

State of matter One of the forms that a substance can take, depending on its temperature and pressure.

Substrate The particular molecule on which an enzyme acts.

Thermodynamics The study of how heat and other forms of energy are converted.

Voltage The force that pushes electrons through an electric circuit.

Wavelength The distance measured from the peak or trough of one wave to the peak or trough of the next.

FURTHER RESEARCH

Books

Atkins, P. W. *The Periodic Kingdom: A Journey into the Land of Chemical Elements.* New York, NY: Barnes & Noble Books, 2007.

Bendick, J., and Wiker, B. *The Mystery of the Periodic Table (Living History Library).* Bathgate, ND: Bethlehem Books, 2003.

Berg, J. *Biochemistry.* New York, NY: W. H. Freeman, 2006.

Brown, T. E. *et al. Chemistry: The Central Science.* Englewood Cliffs, NJ: Prentice Hall, 2008.

Cobb, C., and Fetterolf, M. L. *The Joy of Chemistry: The Amazing Science of Familiar Things.* Amherst, NY: Prometheus Books, 2010.

Davis, M. *et al. Modern Chemistry.* New York, NY: Holt, 2008.

Gray, Theodore. *Theo Gray's Mad Science: Experiments You Can Do at Home—But Probably Shouldn't.* New York, NY: Black Dog & Leventhal Publishers, 2009.

Greenberg A. *From Alchemy to Chemistry in Picture and Story.* Hoboken, NJ: Wiley, 2007.

Herr, N., and Cunningham, J. *Hands-on Chemistry Activities with Real-Life Applications.* Hoboken, NJ: Jossey-Bass, 2002.

Karukstis, K. K., and Van Hecke, G. R. *Chemistry Connections: The Chemical Basis of Everyday Phenomena.* Burlington, MA: Academic Press, 2003.

Lehninger, A., Cox, M., and Nelson, D. *Lehninger's Principles of Biochemistry.* New York, NY: W. H. Freeman, 2008.

LeMay, E. *et al. Chemistry: Connections to Our Changing World.* New York, NY: Prentice Hall (Pearson Education), 2002.

Levere, T. H. *Transforming Matter: A History of Chemistry from Alchemy to the Buckyball.* Baltimore, MD: The Johns Hopkins University Press, 2001.

Oxlade, C. *Elements and Compounds (Chemicals in Action).* Chicago, IL: Heinemann, 2008.

Poynter, M. *Marie Curie: Discoverer of Radium (Great Minds of Science).* Berkeley Heights, NJ: Enslow Publishers, 2007.

Saunders, N. *Fluorine and the Halogens.* Chicago, IL: Heinemann Library, 2005.

Shevick, E., and Wheeler, R. *Great Scientists in Action: Early Life, Discoveries, and Experiments.* Carthage, IL: Teaching & Learning Company, 2004.

Stwertka, A. *A Guide to the Elements.* New York, NY: Oxford University Press, 2002.

Thompson, B. T. *Illustrated Guide to Home Chemistry Experiments: All Lab, No Lecture.* Sebastopol, CA: O'Reilly Media, 2008.

Tiner, J. H. *Exploring the World of Chemistry: From Ancient Metals to High-Speed Computers.* Green Forest, AZ: Master Books, 2000.

Trombley, L., and Williams, F. *Mastering the Periodic Table: 50 Activities on the Elements.* Portland, ME: Walch, 2002.

Walker, P., and Wood, E. *Crime Scene Investigations: Real-life Science Labs for Grades 6–12.* Hoboken, NJ: Jossey-Bass, 2002.

Wilbraham, A., *et al. Chemistry.* New York, NY: Prentice Hall (Pearson Education), 2001.

Woodford, C., and Clowes, M. *Routes of Science: Atoms and Molecules.* San Diego, CA: Blackbirch Press, 2004.

Web sites

The Art and Science of Bubbles
www.sdahq.org/sdakids/bubbles
Information and activities about bubbles.

Chemical Achievers
www.chemheritage.org/classroom/chemach/index.html
Biographical details about leading chemists and their discoveries.

The Chemistry of Fireworks
library.thinkquest.org/15384/chem/chem.htm
Information on the chemical reactions that occur when a firework explodes.

Chemistry: The Periodic Table Online
www.webelements.com
Detailed information about elements.

Chemistry Tutor
library.thinkquest.org/2923
A series of Web pages that help with chemistry assignments.

Chem4Kids
www.chem4Kids.com
Includes sections on matter, atoms, elements, and biochemistry.

Chemtutor Elements
www.chemtutor.com/elem.htm
Information on a selection of the elements.

Eric Weisstein's World of Chemistry
scienceworld.wolfram.com/chemistry
Chemistry information divided into eight broad topics, from chemical reactions to quantum chemistry.

General Chemistry Help
chemed.chem.purdue.edu/genchem
General information on chemistry plus movie clips of key concepts.

IUPAC
www.iupac.org
Web site of the International Union of Pure and Applied Chemistry.

Molecular Models
chemlabs.uoregon.edu/GeneralResources/models/models.html
A site that explains the use of molecular models.

New Scientist
www.newscientist.com/home.ns
Online science magazine providing general news on scientific developments.

The Physical Properties of Minerals
mineral.galleries.com/minerals/physical.htm
Methods for identifying minerals.

Scientific American
www.sciam.com
Latest news on developments in science and technology.

Virtual Laboratory: Ideal Gas Laws
zebu.uoregon.edu/nsf/piston.html
University of Oregon site showing simulation of ideal gas laws.

INDEX

Words and page numbers in **bold type** indicate main references to the various topics. Page numbers in *italic* refer to illustrations; those underlined refer to definitions. Page numbers in brackets indicate box features.

A

absolute zero <u>40</u>, 41, *41*
acids 15
actinides *6–7*
activated complex <u>42</u>
activation energy <u>42</u>, 44–5
active site <u>51</u>
adsorption 49, <u>51</u>
alcohol (12), 13
alkali metals *6–7*, 7
alkaline-earth metals *6–7*
amino acids 51
ammonia 46, 46–7, (47)
amylase 51
anions 10
anodes 55, 56, <u>56</u>
atomic number <u>60</u>
atoms 4, <u>7</u>, *8–9*, 22
  bonds 9–10
Avogadro, Amedeo 19
Avogadro's number 19

B

bases 15
batteries 55–6
  car (33)
  dry *54–5*, (54)
  rechargeable 56
  see also voltaic cells
Bernoulli, Daniel (25)
Bohr model of electrons orbiting 8
boiling point 10
bonds <u>26</u>
  chemical 8–13, 25–6, 31
  covalent 8, 11–12
  ionic 8, 10
  metallic 8, 12–13
Bosch, Carl (47)
Boyle, Robert (15)
Boyle's law (15)
burning *4*, 20–1, *20–1*, 33

C

calorimeters, types of 28, (29), (30), <u>31</u>
carbohydrates 6
carbon dioxide 5
catalase 51
catalysts <u>42</u>, 43, 46, **48–53**
  homogeneous/heterogeneous 49
catalytic converters 49–50, *50*, (50)
cathodes 55, 56, <u>56</u>
cations 10
Celsius scale (41)
chemical bonds 8–13, 25–6, 31

chemical changes 20–2, (20)
chemical equations 17–19, <u>17</u>
chemical formula <u>17</u>
chemical reactions 4–7, (5), <u>7</u>, *14*
  combination reactions 14
  combustion reactions 14, 16–17
  decomposition reactions 15
  displacement reactions 15
  endothermic reactions 26–7, *26*, <u>26</u>, 45
  energy in 20–7, 31
  exothermic reactions 26–7, <u>26</u>, 45
  heat and 28–35
  ingredients 5
  life and (4)
  neutralization reactions 15
  redox reactions 14, 15–16, *17*, 54, 56
  types of 14–19
chemical symbols <u>17</u>
coefficient <u>17</u>
cold packs 33–4
combination reactions 14
combustion reactions 14, 16–17
compounds 5–6, *6*, 19
  covalent 11–12
  ionic 10
  organic 12
conservation of energy, law of 27, 35
copper *12*
covalent bonds 8, 11–12
covalent compounds 11–12
covalent molecules 11
cracking 48, *48–9*
crystal lattice (23)
crystals 10

D

Dalton, John (9)
decomposition reactions 15
diamond 11–12
displacement reactions 15
dissolve <u>14</u>
DNA (deoxyribonucleic acid) 53, 58–9

E

Einstein, Albert 61
electrochemistry 54–7
electrodes 54–5, <u>56</u>
electrolysis 56
electrolyte liquid <u>56</u>
electrolytic cells 56–7
electromagnetic radiation (34), <u>35</u>
electromagnetic spectrum (34)
electronegativity 10
electrons 5, (11), 54
  energy levels 8–9
  location of 8
  number of 9
  octet rule 9
electron shells 8–9

electroplating 57
electrorefining 57
elements 4, <u>7</u>
  radioactive 58
  types of 9–10
endothermic reactions 26–7, *26*, <u>26</u>, 45
energy 4, 6, <u>22</u>, *30–1*, 61
  in chemical reactions 20–7, 31
  energy levels 8–9
  entropy vs 37
  from food *28–9*
  Gibbs free energy 37–9, <u>40</u>
  law of conservation of 27, 35
enthalpy change 35, <u>35</u>, 37–9
entropy 36–41, *36–7*, (37), *39*, <u>40</u>
  vs energy 37
  in open systems 40–1
enzymes 51, <u>51</u>
  lock-and-key mechanism 52
  maltase *52*
  in technology 52–3
  temperature and (52)
equilibrium 45–6, (45)
  moving the equilibrium point 46
ethanol 13
ethers (12), 13
exothermic reactions 26–7, <u>26</u>, 45

F

Fahrenheit scale (41)
Faraday, Michael (56)
fission <u>60</u>
fission reactions 60, *60*, 61
forward reactions 46
fossil fuels 17
fuel cells 57
fusion reactions 60–1, *61*

G

gas laws 23–4
Gibbs, Willard 37
Gibbs free energy 37–9, <u>40</u>
glucose 51

H

Haber, Fritz (47)
Haber-Bosch process (47), 48
half-life <u>60</u>
heat
  and chemical reactions 28–35
  flow of 25, 39
  heat capacity <u>31</u>, (31)
  heat energy <u>26</u>
  heat of reaction 28
helium *18*, 19
Herapath, John (25)
Hess, Germain Henri 35
Hess's law 35
hydrocarbons 16–17
hydrogen 4, *6–7*

I

infrared (heat) radiation (34)
inhibitor <u>51</u>
internal energy 35, <u>35</u>
ionic bonds 8, 10
ionic compounds 10
ions 10
iron 21, *21*
isomers (12), 13
isotopes 59–60, <u>60</u>

J

Joule, James Prescott (25)

K

Kelvin, William Thomson, Lord 41
Kelvin scale <u>40</u>, (41)
kinetic energy 21, <u>22</u>, (24)
kinetic theory <u>22</u>, 23, 24, (25)

L

lactase 51
lactose intolerance 51
lanthanides *6–7*
Le Châtelier, Henri Louis 46
Le Châtelier's principle 46–7
light, visible (34)

M

matter 4, <u>7</u>
  state of <u>26</u>
Maxwell, James Clerk (25)
melting point 10
metal(s) *6–7*, <u>8</u>, 9, 57
metallic bonds 8, 12–13
metalloids *6–7*, <u>8</u>, 10
methane 20–1
microstate <u>40</u>
molecular mass 19
molecules 4, <u>22</u>
  covalent 11
  moving 22–3, 42–3, *43*
  sizes of (23)

N

neutralization reactions 15
neutrons 5
Newton, Isaac (25)
noble gases *6–7*
nonmetals *6–7*, <u>8</u>, 9–10
nuclear equations 61
nuclear power plants (59)
nuclear radiation 58–9
nuclear reactions 14, **58–61**
nucleus 5

O

orbitals 8
organic compounds 12
ozone layer *22*

P

periodic table *6–7*, 7
photosynthesis (4), 26–7
pH (potential hydrogen) 16
potential energy 30–3, *33*, *34–5*, <u>35</u>

precipitate <u>14</u>, 15
products 5, <u>26</u>, 44, *44*
propanols (12), 13
protein <u>51</u>
protons 5

Q

quantum mechanical model of electron location 8

R

radiation
  electromagnetic (34), <u>35</u>
  nuclear 58–9
radioactive decay 58, 59–60, <u>60</u>
reactants 5, <u>26</u>
reaction curves 44, *44*
reaction rates 42–7, *42*, (43), <u>46</u>
redox reactions 14, 15–16, *17*, 54, 56
respiration (4)
reverse reaction 46
reversible reaction <u>46</u>
rusting 21, *21*, 31

S

silicon dioxide (sand) *11*, 12
sodium chloride (salt) 10, (11), 19, *39*
solute <u>14</u>
solution <u>14</u>
solvent <u>14</u>
specific heat capacity <u>31</u>
spontaneous reaction <u>35</u>
state of matter <u>26</u>
strong nuclear force 58
subatomic particles 5–6
substrate <u>51</u>
sugars 51

T

temperature 24–5, *25*
  entropy and 40–1
thermocouples (27)
thermodynamics <u>26</u>
  first law 27, 35, 39
  second law 39–40
thermometers (27)
Thomson, William, Lord Kelvin 41
transition metals *6–7*

U

ultraviolet radiation (34)

V

van der Waals forces 12
Volta, Alessandro 54
voltage <u>56</u>
voltaic cells 54–5

W

wavelength <u>35</u>
work 29–30

Y

yeasts 48, *49*